THE GIRL OF DORCHA WOOD

THE GIRL OF DORCHA WOOD

DAUGHTER OF ERABEL ~ BOOK ONE

KRISTIN WARD

The Girl of Dorcha Wood
Daughter of Erabel Series, Book 1
By Kristin Ward

Editing by David Taylor
Cover Image by JD, JDCoverDesigns

ISBN 978-1-7327923-5-7

Visit https://www.kristinwardauthor.com/

To those who hear the forest calling.

PROLOGUE

When the slaughter had come to its grisly end, they fled. Those who remained, took themselves into hidden recesses scattered across many lands. They mourned the dead and counted the living. In exile, they waited. They grew cold and hardened. Bitter and powerful.

As years turned to decades, they bred. Bred hatred and bred numbers. Until both swelled beyond the ability to contain them.

Then prophecy whispered her arrival upon the wind.

CHAPTER ONE

The sound of blades striking in the violent rhythms of battle rang through the forest, slicing through the air as surely as they cut through flesh. Songbirds fled, while squirrels, shrews, and voles cowered and burrowed beneath bracken or underground, escaping whatever threat had shattered the harmony of Dorcha Wood. Drawn to the commotion, Fiadh ran beneath branches of hawthorn and willow. Her bare feet muffled by the rotted leaves blanketing the forest floor. Keeping to the shadows, she darted among the underbrush, bunching her coarse woolen dress in her hands to keep from tripping as she leaped over fallen logs and moss-covered rocks. The clash of steel, followed by angry bellows, pierced the air, pulling her faster along her disjointed route.

A break in the trees revealed her first glimpse of three men in heated combat, swords swinging in deadly arcs as bodies dodged and metal deflected. Slowing her pace, Fiadh crept closer and ducked behind a large oak bordering the meadow. Using a low branch as cover, she peered at the scene before her. Two men circled a third, their steps cautious, legs crisscrossing in a macabre dance. On the ground lay a fourth individual. Marcas' eyes were fixed in an empty stare, his life having clearly bled out upon the grass.

Fiadh looked back at the battle unfolding in the ordinarily peaceful meadow beyond the tree line. Blood and sweat covered the skin and scraggly beard of the man at the center of the attack, obscuring his features and age, but not enough that Fiadh knew she had never seen him before. The others were regrettably familiar. Jarvis and Hamish were part of Lord Darragh Baoill's guard and, along with their now deceased comrade, were known for their cruelty and abuse of the villagers of Felmore. Fiadh recalled watching from the safety of the shadows of the forest as they flogged peasants until their backs were nothing but strips of open flesh. Or as they snatched women who had the misfortune of traveling through the recesses of the village unaccompanied, dragging them into dark corners where all she heard were faint cries. It would please her to see them cut down by the stranger they circled, their blades darting in and out in search of an opening.

Fiadh watched the man at the center of the battle. He wore a tunic of dark cloth embellished with threads of silver embroidery that glinted beneath leather armor, complete with pauldrons and bracers, its chest piece carved with a crest she didn't recognize. Muscular legs, swathed in thick woolen chausses, scissored as his blade whistled through the air in practiced rhythms. But with every strike, his sword slowed as though dragged toward the earth itself. The force of his blows waned. Peering closely, she saw blood streaming down his left arm and a large gash above his knee that looked so deep it surprised her he could stand much less fight. A wave of pity at the stranger's fate washed over Fiadh as she saw Jarvis and Hamish pass a signal to one another before launching a coordinated assault from both sides. The man's body twisted and darted, sword slashing through the air with such swift movements it became a blur. Grunts of exertion mixed with yelps of pain filled the air as blades found their mark. The small battle soaked the meadow grasses in thick clots of blood. She could smell it, tangy and metallic.

Sucking in a breath, Fiadh watched the stranger fall to one knee, Jarvis having jabbed his blade into the man's upper thigh. She knew it was over then and felt sadness for the poor soul they now taunted, sharp points stabbing into his back and sides, not enough to kill, only to cause pain. The man's head bowed, chest heaving. Hamish raised his sword, arms extended to their full length, then cleaved downward for the death blow. Before the blade tore through the man's neck, the stranger bent forward and thrust his sword upward and into Hamish's belly. He twisted it viciously and ripped the metal out so forcefully Fiadh almost retched at the sight of what came with it. Hamish's eyes bugged, and his mouth fell open. He dropped his sword to clutch his middle, stumbling like a drunk. Blood spurted from the wound in gushes, slipping past his fingers as he crashed to the ground.

Jarvis screamed, "You bastard!" lunging at the man who now tilted his body to the side. His knee dug into the ground, creating a small rut. Swinging his arm in a horizontal sweep, he severed Jarvis' left leg mid-thigh. Shrieks filled the air, drowning out the twisting and writhing of

Hamish, still vainly clutching at the bloody, wormy mass spilling from his stomach. The carnage in the space of a few seconds was appalling. Fiadh's heart hammered in her chest. She had never witnessed such brutality and wanted nothing more than to run, but her body had frozen, locked in fear so primal she could only stare.

Staggering to his feet, the stranger stood over Jarvis and watched dispassionately as the man wriggled on the ground, clutching his severed limb. Lifting his sword, the stranger paused, tip pointed above Jarvis' chest for just a moment, before plunging it into his body. The muted sounds of butchery traveled to Fiadh's ears and she shuddered, gaze fixed on the scene as though anchored. Jarvis yelped, twitched, then grew still.

"Who are you?" Hamish whispered as the man approached, sword plastered with the blood of his friend. She realized Hamish had only moments to live as he contemplated the man who would take his life. Perhaps they had thought this stranger would be an easy target, like so many others before him. Or maybe there had been some minor slight they had deemed worthy of blood. Whatever came before this carnage, the stranger was now ending it. On his terms.

Looking down at Hamish, he said, "I am your reckoning," before driving the blade into Hamish's heart.

Fiadh's body unlocked. She covered her mouth to muffle a gasp and watched the stranger sway, sword hanging limply in his right hand. She shifted her weight, relieving the numbness creeping up her leg, and accidentally slid her foot onto a brittle twig that gave way with a loud snap. The stranger glanced up through tracks of blood splatter, tired but alert, and scanned the wood, stopping when he found her. Lunging forward in an awkward gait, he came for her, his sword gripped in fingers caked in gore and sweat. Fiadh scrambled backward, falling hard when her feet tangled on the hem of her dress. Caring nothing for any noise he made, the man blundered through the trees, murder in his glare.

She tried to scream, but fear strangled her voice. Sprawled on the forest floor, surrounded by the woods she had known since childhood, Fiadh watched as the man stalked toward her. Dorcha Wood awoke as he passed beneath the bowers of ancient trees. Branches reached for him, limbs twisting into claws that stretched woody fingers to halt his progress. He brushed them away and stumbled forward, stopping just beyond her prone form, sword raised though she saw his arms tremble with the effort. Fiadh looked into the face of death as he stood over her in a mask of blackening blood.

His eyes, a brilliant blue within his grisly features, stared into her. From somewhere close by, she caught a soft whistling sound that matched the rhythms of her frantic heartbeat. Fiadh saw indecision flash in the stranger's face. The sword wavered in the air, its wicked blade tilting this way and that, before slowly lowering, its point digging into the dark soil. Air whooshed out of her lungs, stopping the strange whistling noise she had heard only moments before. Digging her heels into the soft earth, she struggled to sit up, holding out her hands.

Finding her voice, she pleaded, "I'm not one of them."

The stranger nodded slowly, but offered no response other than the motion. As moments passed, during which her heart regained its normal rhythm, Fiadh relaxed her muscles, anchoring herself to the earth, feeling its energy course through her in calming waves. Closing her eyes briefly, she sent pulses of thought and intention to this outsider, the same feelings and messages she would send to the timid fauna who found their way to her within the depths of Dorcha Wood. Though Fiadh felt no tangible response from his mind, she opened her eyes, feeling assured he wouldn't harm her, and gradually got to her feet. From her view of the brutal skirmish, she hadn't realized how tall he was and now found herself craning her neck to stare into his travel-worn face. He looked down at her, his breath coming in pants, like that of an animal who had run too far, too fast. She watched his chest heave, the thick pads of muscle under his tunic straining, sensing he was going to pass out if he stood much longer. As if to affirm her suspicion, his knees buckled, sword falling to the side with a thump.

Her hands reached forward out of habit before she pulled them back and asked softly, "Who are you?"

He looked up at her, face filled with pain and weariness. "Gideon."

CHAPTER TWO

Gideon blinked rapidly, his eyes becoming glassy, as Fiadh started toward him with slow, deliberate steps, as though he were a wounded bear. Wary of his intent and ready to flee, she marked his movements, pausing when his body shifted. The man shook his head, his skin growing pale beneath the gore and his unkempt beard, before turning a ghastly white. She had seen the look before as a young girl when her mother worked to save a woman whose birthing had gone badly. That event hadn't ended well. The new mother bled out on the bedding amidst the silence of a babe who never took his first breath.

The healer in her reached toward this stranger, fingers extending to his neck to feel the thrum of his pulse. Gideon jerked away, clumsily toppling to the side before righting himself onto his knees with unsteady hands.

"I won't hurt you," Fiadh said, lacing her voice with the same soothing inflection and underlying intent she used on the timorous wild things she coaxed to her hand.

He looked at her arm, trying to focus, and then into her

features before pitching forward and landing facedown at her feet. Fiadh stood in shock for a moment, thinking he was dead, but beneath his bloodstained clothes, she detected the shallow rise and fall of his chest. Crouching next to his still form, she took his measure, feeling the beat of his heart. Sinking to her knees, she wedged her hands under his large body, lifting with great effort, trying to turn him onto his back. It took several minutes to wrestle his form to its side and then gently roll him. Stretching over his body, she cupped the back of his head and let it rest on the leaf-littered ground.

The wound on his left arm just above the bracer had stopped bleeding, leaving dark tracks on his skin that were beginning to discolor to a blackened crust, while the small wounds on his torso and back were minor enough to be ignored for now. Gideon's leg was a different story. There were two injuries to his thigh, one on the inner portion close to his knee and the second on his outer upper leg. They would all need stitching. Hopping up, Fiadh dashed into the woods, pulling a small blade, one she used to collect plants, from the leather sheath hanging on her braided belt, and began casting about for comfrey, yarrow, bleeding heart, and lichen to make a poultice.

All around her, the forest groaned, growing dark as the uppermost branches bent inward, blocking the light. The creaking of trees filled the quiet with haunting sounds that had frightened countless wanderers from its depths, sending them racing from the woods with stories of the evil lurking there. Fiadh paused and closed her eyes, stretching her senses into Dorcha Wood, soothing the life that beat with fierce anger until the forest let out a sigh as branches shifted and settled.

Once she had what she needed, she took the plants to a nearby stream and smashed them with rocks to grind them into a thick pulp before tearing off three strips of her dress and folding a handful of the mass into each of them. After soaking the cloths in the water for a few moments, she ran back to Gideon and secured the larger poultice on the worst of the wounds, binding it around his thigh before securing it with a knot, then moving on to the other lacerations. When the poultices were in place, she cast about for a horse to transport him to her hut deep in the wood. Her mother was best with a needle and would make quick work of the sewing.

The only horses to be found were those of the stranger's attackers, their poor state the best indication of whom they belonged. Taking one of them could lead Lord Darragh's soldiers to her door, and that was not something she could risk. Slipping the tack from the dead men's mounts, she tossed it onto the ground, then whacked their rumps, sending them into a gallop. If the fates were with them, they would not be found, free to live the rest of their lives away from the cruel whips whose marks had left years of scars upon their bowed backs. Dragging the saddles and harnesses into the woods, she covered them with a layer of debris, reluctant to do a more thorough job as Gideon could conceivably be on a swift road to death the more time that passed. Turning in a slow circle, she mulled over her options, acknowledging the strangeness of the outsider having no mount but brushing the thought aside when it was apparent he had traveled on foot, or the animal was well and truly gone. It became clear there was only one natural course of action given the man's condition.

She fashioned a makeshift litter from branches and strips of bark from a sapling. Placing the contraption next to Gideon, she slowly rolled him over, grunting with effort as his dead weight worked against her until she finally managed to wrestle his body onto it. Sliding his sword into its sheath, she tucked it against his side, letting his weight hold it in place. Fiadh stood, nodding to herself before arching her neck back and sending out a rolling trill through the trees. She cocked her head and listened, calling out again with a noise resembling an odd collection of bird-songs. In minutes, she was rewarded with the sound of hooves moving through the vegetation. Fiadh stood patiently as a beautiful buck, with antlers extending outward the entire length of a man, walked toward her, bowing his head when he was an arm's distance.

"Hello, Niall," she crooned, extending her hand to stroke the buck's velvety nose. "I can use your strong back today, my friend."

The deer's liquid eyes bore into her, seeming to take in every word and make meaning of it. It had always been like this. Wild things found their way to Fiadh, and she could communicate with many of them through touch, thought, and words. She had often teased her mother, Riona, that she must be a changeling, one of the Aos Sí who had lived in these lands before they were hunted down and slaughtered. Riona scoffed at such nonsense, though at times, there was an underlying current of fear or worry under the surface. Something Fiadh had never been able to explore, being cut off at the mention of it.

Those taboo peoples were relics of a tragic past whose mark on the world was ruthlessly obliterated. Lord Darragh's grandfather, Magnar, had led a crusade against the elves, running them to ground, massacring entire families who dared to live alongside powerful men who had claimed the world as their own. At least that's how the story went. To preserve that awful legacy, the current lord had long ago outlawed storytelling and artwork glorifying the Aos Sí, even the myths of little people and those who lived beneath the sea. Even so, Fiadh had still heard stories in snippets of forbidden tales told in quiet corners of the village while she hid and listened.

The forest was utterly absent of their kind by the time Fiadh was born. However, perhaps there remained a part of them still lingering in Dorcha Wood, like a stain, keeping villagers away for fear of the things that dwelled therein, all those terrifying stories of monsters and magic. Mother had said that was why they lived in this place. Away from the prying stares of the people of Felmore. In the heart of a forest which bore its past like a shield, protecting those within it. Of course, being a practitioner of healing arts meant her mother had been somewhat of an outcast, to begin with, though people still sought out her medicines when in need, just not within the boundaries of Dorcha Wood. It was better to be apart from watchful eyes and wagging tongues in these times. At seventeen years, Fiadh had no memory of life outside the wood and couldn't imagine leaving the forest's tranquility for the realm of men.

Reaching out a hand, Fiadh curled her fingers across the silky face of the buck, whispering calming words as his body twitched and nostrils flared at the scent of blood, ready for flight should the slightest noise alarm him. She slipped a hand around his ear to tug gently at an antler. Leading him in a half-circle, she positioned the deer so that it planted its hind feet at Gideon's head and the front of the litter. Using long strips of saplings she had braided into a rope, she secured it around the buck like a harness for a plow horse. Holding the fibers in place against Niall's chest, she urged him onward.

"To my home," she murmured. Niall lurched forward, delicate hooves thumping on the ground in a slow rhythm. He had been to her home numerous times, and Fiadh smiled as he turned his body in a north-westward direction. "You know the ways through the forest better than I ever will."

The journey was slow. Gideon's limp body bounced with each step, frequently threatening to topple off the litter. Finally, her wattle and daub hut, with smoke curling from a tiny opening in the thatched roof, came into view. Fiadh let out a sigh of relief, glad to be where her mother could take stock of Gideon's injuries and work her healing magic. Leading Niall to the rough wooden door, she stroked his back, sliding the loop of fibers off of him.

"Thank you, my friend."

Niall turned his head, his massive antlers sweeping over her. Huffing softly, he nudged her forehead with his wet nose before bolting into the forest.

Riona unlatched the door and swung it open, cocking an eyebrow when she took in the prone man on the ground. She was an extraordinarily handsome woman, despite the smattering of wrinkles framing her face and the streaks of grey accenting red hair that looked like the pale shades of a sunrise against her lightly freckled skin. Fiadh was dark where her mother was light, with hair so black there were no strands of brown to mar its perfection, and skin which glowed with a luminescence Riona liked to claim was the result of her daughter's wildness. And within these youthful features were eyes, striking against her fair skin and dark hair, of such a crystalline green brilliance they glowed.

"Where did you find him?" Riona asked, frowning and setting aside the bundle of herbs she had been binding to hang from the rafters. Gone were the days when Mother was surprised by what Fiadh brought home. Although, those who found themselves at their threshold had been nothing more than wild things for years. Once, Fiadh had brought a girl who'd had the unlucky fortune of ending up at the hands of Darragh's ruthless guards. Riona had reluctantly allowed it, perhaps moved by the sight of one so innocent falling prey to the violence of men. They had sheltered her for days, using every medicinal herb to mend her body, but healing her mind was beyond their skill, and they had let her go, leaving her wandering toward the village just beyond the edge of the wood. And since that time, there had been no one. There was danger in helping those whose words could travel, be heard, and be acted upon.

"In the eastern meadow. He was attacked by three of Lord Darragh's men." Fiadh saw her mother's refusal before it was uttered. "I know the risks, but no one will know."

Riona pursed her lips. "Fiadh, we have spoken of this. An animal is one thing, but a grown man? And what of Lord Darragh's men? Where do you think his soldiers will come looking to seek vengeance?"

"I couldn't leave him, Mother. He..." Fiadh floundered,

trying to find the words. How could she explain the pull she felt for this stranger as she watched him fend off those monsters?

"What?" Riona asked, her heart beating fiercely. *They'll come for her*, her mind screamed, dredging up images of her husband's broken body mixed with cries of anguish for the loss of her son.

Lifting her arms in a limp gesture, Fiadh said, "I had to help him."

"You know nothing of this stranger. How can you think to bring him here?" Riona snapped, her eyes flashing to Gideon.

She doesn't understand the danger, Riona's mind shouted, while another part of her begged her to tell Fiadh of her past, all of the things she had kept hidden to keep her safe. All her daughter knew was the story she had told her of a terrible storm that had taken the lives of her father and brother. Fiadh knew nothing of Darragh's part in their deaths. She knew nothing of who she really was and why her true identity was such a risk. But, this was not the time, she realized, staring down at the prone form of a man her daughter had felt compelled to save. Perhaps, she was destined to find him. For all she knew, he was some piece of the puzzle that defined her daughter.

"Please, Mother." Fiadh watched Riona fold her arms across her chest and stare down at the man. "Just help me see to him. What's the harm in that?"

After a few protracted moments, Riona nodded. "All right. But one night only, and then he must be on his way, healed or no."

Fiadh's shoulders sagged in relief. She knew, having

watched the battle, Gideon's wounds were no trifling thing. One day of Mother's healing ways would not suffice. But she would let that realization come when it would, sure her mother would not send him off before he was ready.

"And the men who attacked him?" Riona asked, leaning down to look at the stranger at her feet. "Did they see you?"

"Nay, Mother," Fiadh said. "And even if they had, he cut them down," waving her hand at Gideon's still form.

Her mother always worried that one day she would find herself in a situation she couldn't escape. It was not unheard of for a woman to go missing.

Lord Darragh Baoill came from a long line of manor lords who had ruled the fiefdom since the elven wars. When King Stephan Laoghaire was crowned, Darragh had renewed his pledge to the kingdom, vowing fealty to a venal man whose deviant behavior was well known. It was even rumored King Stephan had killed his father for the crown, though such things were whispered in secret for fear of reprisal. In Lord Darragh, King Stephan had found a loyal vassal whose disposition matched his own and gave him freedoms over his land his predecessors had never attained in their lifetimes. The greed and cruelty of a few, fed by a man who surrounded himself by those who would do his bidding with no compunction or quarrel, systematically tainted the peaceful hamlet of her mother's childhood. Peasants had become prey, as those whose station was meant to protect became something monstrous.

Riona capitulated. "All right. Help me bring him in, and I will see what can be done."

CHAPTER THREE

Working together, the women hauled Gideon onto a pallet and tugged his leather armor and tunic off as he lay unmoving. Riona looked at her daughter as she eyed the man's trousers. "Turn away, Fiadh."

Doing as she was told, Fiadh spun around, fiddling with her braided belt as she listened to her mother's grunts of exertion as she stripped the knight of his boots and leggings.

"You may assist me now," Riona said when she had finished. Fiadh joined her, blushing at the sight of a naked man, eyes darting to the folded cloth her mother had placed over his groin. "He is just a man, like any other, Daughter."

"Aye, Mother," Fiadh whispered. She squared her shoulders and fetched a bowl of water and cleansing herbs.

They washed his body, peeling off layers of blood and grime to reveal old scars and new injuries while noting the more superficial wounds that would not require a needle. It was a soothing task, the rhythms of their hands becoming mesmerizing. Soak, ring, swipe, rinse. For many minutes, the only sounds in their single-room hut were those of their work intertwined with muted breaths. And then Riona began a quiet chant, calling to the Great Mother, Danu, asking for her blessings to heal the man. Fiadh joined her and their voices, pitched low, filled the quiet before softly fading to silence.

Riona regarded Gideon's freshly revealed face, noting the youthfulness under the ragged beard that reflected travel and hard living. "I haven't seen this man before."

Fiadh took in his features, the strong jaw beneath a thick layer of beard and the slight curve on the bridge of his nose where it looked like an old break had not healed right. Though weathered from the elements, his cheeks were free of wrinkles. A thin raised scar ran down the left side of his face from his temple before disappearing under a patch of beard. Sweeps of dark lashes and eyebrows, devoid of the grayness of age, stood out against his chapped skin. Peering at him, she had to wonder if he was much younger than he appeared. Despite the rough soldier's life stamped upon his visage, Gideon was a striking man, tall and muscled with thick, brown hair hanging past his shoulders. She took in the braids on either side of his face, recognizing them for symbols of war.

Holding one of the woven masses in her hand, she looked at her mother. "Do you think he was in a battle before he found himself here?"

Riona lifted her gaze from the wound she had been inspecting and took the man's hair in her hands. "It would appear he was headed to one at the very least, but I have not heard of any skirmishes nearby. He had no horse?"

Fiadh shook her head.

"Strange for such a one to have traveled on foot, alone…" Riona's voice faded.

Fiadh watched her mother's mind working, seeing a spark of unease crease her brow, but nothing more was said. Dropping the braid, Riona stood and fetched a needle and thread. Returning to her place on the dirt floor, she commanded Fiadh, "Hold his leg while I sew."

Nodding, Fiadh leaned over opposite her mother and clamped her hands onto Gideon's heavily muscled leg, pressing firmly, as Riona pierced the ragged edges of his skin. He twitched as the needle tugged his flesh but never woke. Once each wound was sewn, and the less severe assessed, Riona covered them with a thick paste, binding the more critical injuries with clean rags. Sitting back on her heels, she said, "That's all I can do for him."

Fiadh rinsed her hands in a bowl of water and wiped them with a rough cloth. "Do you think he'll live?"

"He has a fair chance, though he's weak, and it's not just from the attack."

"What do you mean?" Fiadh asked, considering Gideon's body as though she could somehow discern what her mother spoke of.

Bending over the man, Riona peeled back an eyelid. "Do you see the yellow in the whites of his eye?" Fiadh nodded. "He is not well, whether from illness or poison, and his injuries may take a toll he can't recover from."

Though Fiadh didn't know this man, it saddened her to see someone brought low at the hands of those who would not hesitate to kill the innocent alongside the guilty. But she knew enough to understand some could not be saved. Taking heart in the knowledge that she had done all she could, Fiadh left Gideon to heal or succumb by the heat of the small fire.

Slipping into the forest, Fiadh went back to the scene of the attack. Peering through the branches bordering the meadow, she could see the three guardsmen lying where they had fallen, their bodies growing stiff in the cool, autumn air. Scanning the landscape in front of her, she worried about Darragh's retaliation should he come upon this scene. With three of his soldiers slain, he would undoubtedly launch a search for the killer and could find Gideon, and she and her mother would be guilty of harboring a man who had attacked the lord's guards. That is if they dared to venture into the woods at all.

The villagers of Felmore were a superstitious lot, and Dorcha Wood was considered an evil place of ancient elven magic. Darragh's guards were no different in their beliefs, but happening upon the corpses of their men could sway them enough to enter the forest and seek vengeance. After all, despite their fears, they knew it was men and steel which had prevailed in the Great War, not magic and witchcraft. It was a frightening notion.

Mother had told her they had deserted the village for the woods' safety after her father and brother had died. A widow with a young girl living within the boundaries of Felmore was at risk of being preyed upon by Darragh's men. So, they had left that world. It had happened so long ago Fiadh could not recall ever having lived within the confines of that place. She could not remember the faces of her father or brother either.

Shaking off the past, Fiadh looked at the trees that sheltered her. If Darragh's men found the bodies and invaded their haven with bloodlust, what would become of her and Mother?

A dark thought entered Fiadh's mind, whispering through her head. She shied away from it at first, horrified even to consider such an action. But the idea wouldn't relent, snaking past her refusal and instinct to shy away from such a notion. Cù-Sìth. She could call upon the pack of Cù-Sìth who lived in the craggy hills deep in the forest. Relics from the past, they traveled their domain in small groups, hunting and raising their offspring far from the world of men. They were the nightmarish beasts mothers of the village told their children of, warning them to keep away from the woods. Every few years, a tale would surface of a sighting or the discovery of the mutilated remains of a foolish soul who had crossed the border of Dorcha Wood. They had never left this place, unlike the Aos Sí, who had used them as ruthless guardians of their kingdom. Instead, they lived on in relative secrecy, their names intertwined with frightening legends whose origins were lost in time.

Fiadh knew the Cù-Sìth as no other did, having long ago felt their presence when roaming the depths of the forest. Theirs was an alien mind compared to the other wild things of Dorcha Wood. She had been drawn to them, her curiosity overriding caution. But nothing could have prepared her for what she saw when they found her.

Remembering that time sent a shiver up Fiadh's spine, the images of that day so clear. They had spat themselves out of the woods. A group of four materializing in a dizzying blur of hulking forms from a line of trees, their bodies becoming defined as they sprang into the light filtering from tall branches of oak and pine. The size of giant bears, the Cù-Sìth bore little resemblance to any natural creature. In bizarre patterns of black and mossy green, thick fur covered enormous canine bodies typified by massive chests and solid limbs, bristling at their shoulders in chaotic spikes before smoothly trailing down their bodies into lengthy tails with long strands of fur that braided itself into a curious knotwork. They had the muzzles of wolves, though much broader with immense jaws. The creature, whose posture indicated leadership, had curled a lip with a soft rumble as she stood immobile, revealing serrated teeth that could slice through bone as easily as flesh. Yellow eyes, stark against dark fur, reflecting an intelligence far beyond any she had encountered outside of the minds of humankind.

Why they did not tear her to pieces on sight as they had in countless stories, she would never know. It had taken all of her courage to stand her ground and reach out to them with her mind, speaking words of friendship and peace. Somehow, the small pack of Cù-Sìth had understood, slowly sinking into the cover of darkness within the shadowy recesses of the woods until it was as though she had imagined them. She had not seen them since that day, but she had felt them, felt their peculiar intellect, and, now and then, the weighted feel of their stares.

Limbs trembling with the knowledge of what she was about to do, Fiadh called to the pack, sending thoughts and images with the sole purpose of finding their strange minds and bringing them to her. Riona would be horrified if she knew what Fiadh was about. Discussing her affinity with nature and her unusual connection with Dorcha Wood always caused a shadow to fall over her mother's face. There were secrets there, buried under layers of avoidance. Fiadh had given up trying to dig them out long ago. It was not worth fighting to pry something out of her mother she would never willingly tell. So, Fiadh kept her secrets. And now she would add another, a wicked secret that reflected a part of her she had rarely faced.

Though it was cool, Fiadh's palms began to sweat, and she rubbed them on the coarse fabric of her dress as she paced, at war with herself but determined to see this through. She had not killed these men, she rationalized. What did it matter if nightmarish beasts consumed them? It would be no different than the scavengers who roamed the landscape, picking at their flesh and tearing it from bone. In the end, the result would be the same, only quicker and without the risk of Darragh's men discovering the remains. Fiadh strode in tight circles, glancing through the trees as time passed, growing more agitated with every second until she was on the cusp of leaving.

They made no sound as they arrived. One moment, birdsong and the scurrying of small things filled the woods and, the next was silenced. Six Cù-Sìth stood a short distance away, their monstrous forms even more frightening than she remembered. Forcing herself to stop pacing, Fiadh walked slowly toward them, projecting confidence she didn't feel as her mind blared red with alarm and an urge to run. The Cù-Sìth remained motionless. Their eyes—yellowed pools of frightening understanding—watched her movements. When she was a couple of steps from the closest animal, she stopped.

The individual came toward her, lowering its huge head to be level with her face. An odd scent filled her nose as the animal's breath huffed from its wide nostrils. Rank and sweet at the same time, the smell enveloped her, making her want to gag at its cloying scent. Swallowing hard, she looked into its endless gaze.

Reining in her fear, Fiadh spoke to the beast from within her mind. *Mankind threatens the forest if these men are found.* She followed this with images of foxes and vultures consuming the dead, with the hope that this would translate into something they could comprehend.

There was no response, not a flicker of understanding. Her heart sank. What if she couldn't communicate with them after all? A low rumbling emanating from the chest of the Cù-Sìth facing her interrupted her thought. Lifting her head to look at him fully, she cleared her mind, inviting his thoughts into hers, and was startled by their clarity.

Men always threaten.

Fiadh nodded, eyes wide with shock. How was this possible? She had never had such a clear connection before. With the forest animals, their communication was more impressions and images than anything genuinely expressive. Marveling at this odd discovery, she sent out a reply. *Aye, but if they find these men, they will come to kill,* she told him.

What do you ask?

Glancing at the bodies that lay beyond the tree line, she turned back to him and stood tall, resolute in the need to keep the lord of Felmore from learning what happened here. *Will you take their bodies?* she asked, while inside, she imagined the Cù-Sìth devouring all evidence of the men until there was nothing left. Truthfully, that had been her idea from the start.

Her errant musing must have been conveyed, and she felt ashamed as the Cù-Sìth's mind touched hers once again. *We do not consume the flesh of man, but we will rid this land of them and protect the forest from those who may come seeking their brethren.*

With no apparent indication to the creatures who stood behind him, the Cù-Sìth stepped forward, his massive body passing by her frozen form less than a hand's length away, followed by the others. He stopped at the edge of the forest, swinging his head toward her as she followed his progress. *I am Vaymi, guardian of Erabel. You may call on us when you have a need, and we will answer.*

Fiadh did not know a place called Erabel. The name had never been part of any histories she had learned or stories she had been told. Perhaps that is what the Cù-Sìth called their territory, for it was clear they were not the mindless beasts of children's stories. *Thank you, Vaymi. I am Fiadh.*

A larger, darker Cù-Sìth separated himself from the pack and stepped forward, his stare pinning her to the ground with such authority she could do nothing but stare. *We know who you are. I am Krulan.*

With that, he turned away, and the six creatures surrounded the fallen guards. Four were chosen through some communication she couldn't see, and they leaned down, mouths opening impossibly large, before closing around the torsos of the men, with one taking Jarvis' severed leg. The soft snapping of bones breaking in their massive jaws as they lifted the corpses made her shudder. The fifth individual was left to cleanse the land, which had grown dark with pools of dried blood, under the watchful eye of Krulan. Digging his massive paws into the ground, he tore up grass and dirt, burrowing into the soil until the darkness of the rich earth blended with the blood. As one, the six Cù-Sìth returned to the forest, melting into the shadows without a sound.

Fiadh stood rooted, staring into the place where the pack had disappeared. It was such an unexpected encounter. While she had hoped they would help erase the evidence of the attack on Gideon, even if that meant the gruesome task of eating the dead, she had not been prepared for the reality of communicating with such an advanced species. It was as disturbing as it was astonishing, and she once again marveled at the secrets the wood kept hidden. Forcefully pulling her mind away from the event, she stepped into the meadow, relieved to see all that remained was overturned earth which could have come from an animal searching for prey hidden beneath the ground. The Cù-Sìth had even taken the fallen men's swords. Within days, the grasses would take over, and there would be no trace of what occurred here, a knowledge that meant safety, not only for the man she had saved but for herself and Riona.

Shaking off the uneasiness of what she had done, Fiadh went back to the site where Gideon had collapsed at her feet and cut a low branch to use as a broom, sweeping dirt and debris into the small ruts caused by his litter as he was dragged. Better to hide all traces, she thought, as she swept back and forth along the route. This was not the first time she had hidden signs of her presence from anyone who may come looking. Life had taught her the importance of covering her tracks. To the people of Felmore, she was a shadow, seen only in glimpses that left the onlooker wondering if their eyes played tricks on them. A living ghost.

By the time Fiadh finished clearing traces of her passing from the forest floor, it had grown dark. Tossing the branch away, she went inside. Riona stood at the hearth, slowly stirring the contents of a large kettle hanging above the flames. The smell of vegetable pottage filled her nostrils, and Fiadh's stomach snarled in anticipation.

"You swept the woods?" her mother asked, spooning out a mouthful to taste.

"Aye." Fiadh didn't add how the Cù-Sìth had carried the bodies away after their unusual communion. "How is he?"

"Feverish," Riona said bluntly. "He's opened his eyes a time or two and thrashed about, muttering of battle and death."

"I picked these thinking you may be running low," Fiadh said, handing Riona bundles of boneset, sage, and lavender. Crouching next to Gideon, she took in his flushed face. Finding a clean rag and bowl, she added willow bark and dipped the folded cloth into the mixture before pressing it to his forehead.

Riona watched her daughter, smiling fondly. "You are a sound healer, Fiadh. It is past time you recognized your gift. You rely too much on me."

Fiadh smiled, pride suffusing her face for a moment. "I still have much to learn."

"Not as much as you think. Come," Riona prodded, "eat

so you can tend to him during the night. You will do no one any good if you wear yourself thin."

Taking the wooden bowl from her mother's hands, Fiadh sat on one of two stools to eat the hearty stew. The warmth of the meal filled her stomach and brought a familiar measure of contentment, as food always managed to elicit. She ate with gusto, scraping the bowl's bottom and edges to finish every morsel before setting it aside to be washed in the nearby creek. Her mother ate more slowly, able to savor while her daughter devoured.

Riona gestured to Gideon. "There is some thick broth left that you could try feeding him."

Fiadh ducked out to wash her dish and spoon before ladling the remnants of the meal into her bowl. Having set aside her supper, Riona nudged Gideon awake and then helped prop up his head and upper body onto Fiadh's folded pallet. Once he was at an appropriate angle, Fiadh dipped her spoon into the thick vegetable broth and put it to his lips as he watched her with half-mast eyes. Nudging them apart, she slipped the spoon into his mouth, carefully spilling the contents onto his tongue. Gideon swallowed instinctively, his throat working visibly as she continued to feed him. It worried her that he was so weak, and she accepted he might not last the night. When the last of the broth was scraped from the bowl, Fiadh removed the bundled pallet and repositioned Gideon so he could sleep. Letting out a soft sigh of thanks, he fell back into slumber.

The two women laid out their mats on the hard floor, Fiadh's next to Gideon so she could assist him during the wee hours should he awaken. Dousing the lantern, the hut was suffused in darkness, aside from the weak light of the moon coming through the thin membrane covering a single opening on one wall.

"Rest, daughter," Riona said, yawning. "If he lives through the night, then he has a chance. If not, then it wasn't meant to be."

"Aye, Mother," she replied, "I will."

Sleep came quickly, as it always did. Fiadh enjoyed a beautiful dreamscape when she was jolted awake by Gideon's arm as he flailed in the throes of a nightmare. Rolling over, she reached for his arms, pinning them to his chest. She knew he should be able to throw her off, but his body was wracked with fever, the muscles of his arms grown weak and limp.

"Doran!" Gideon yelled, his voice hoarse and dry. "Doran!"

Riona leaped from her bedding, swooping down to help her daughter subdue Gideon. He thrashed, vainly trying to throw them off.

"Doran, run! Run!" Gideon cried, his voice growing thinner with each shout. With a sudden gurgle, he went limp, head flopping to the side.

"Is he dead?" Fiadh whispered.

Riona felt for his pulse. "Nay, he's asleep."

Rubbing her hand on her face, Riona sat with a thump, waving her daughter to her side and squeezing her. "We've done what we could. Keep his body cool and try to make him drink."

"Poor man," Fiadh whispered. "I wonder who Doran is."

"If he wakes, you can ask," Riona said and kissed her on

the head before reclining onto her bed. "Rouse me if he takes a bad turn."

"Good sleep, Mother," Fiadh called out quietly before turning her attention to Gideon. His mouth was slack, lips cracked and coated in a thin film of dried spit.

Taking a bowl and cloth, she dipped the edge into the water and squeezed it into his mouth, wiping up the drops that spilled from the corners. It took a few minutes to empty the bowl, and throughout it all, he remained still, aside from the slow bobbing in his neck as he swallowed. The hours of night crept by, slowly fading into dawn. Fiadh, having lost her fight to stay awake, slept curled next to Gideon, her head tucked against his shoulder.

That's how he found her when he woke.

CHAPTER FOUR

Gideon looked about the small dwelling, taking in the herbs hanging from the rafters, the mud-hewn walls, and thatched roof, barely visible in the weak light of morning. It smelled earthy with a hint of something floral, perhaps lavender. The fire in the hearth gave out anemic heat, a few orange embers glowing. He had no memory of this place. The last thing his mind conjured was an ambush in a field and a dim image of a girl in the forest.

A light snore by his head made him turn, and he found himself gazing at the same girl his mind had summoned from fragments of memory. She was in a deep sleep, her dark hair spilling wildly in all directions. There was a black smudge of ash or dirt on her silken cheek below eyelids layered in feathery lashes that rested atop a purplish hue staining her skin, as though she had gone through numerous sleepless nights. Rosy lips, their softly plump shape curving in a perfect bow, were parted, revealing the tips of white teeth. Not a girl after all, but a young woman, perhaps just shy of twenty. Gideon looked at her closely, trying to discern if he had ever seen her before these strange events, but couldn't recall having ever met such a comely woman. Hers wasn't a face or form he would soon forget. Casting his gaze about the tiny hovel once again, he tried to piece together the events that had led him to this place, but they were messy things with no discernable timeline. Gideon's head pounded with the effort, forcing him to give up as his mind swam in a haze of misery.

Someone stirred in a part of the hut he hadn't noticed, making him still his breath and strain to listen. Feet shuffled, followed by a rustling sound. Gideon cracked his lids, enough to see but giving the perception of sleep. The worn hem of a green woolen dress came into view as a woman crept by to stoke the fire, gently placing logs upon the coals. Pouring water from a pitcher into a bowl, she turned and knelt next to him.

"You're awake," she said, her voice soothing and low.

Finding no use in pretending, he looked at her, observing her dampen a cloth before bathing his face. While older than the beauty next to him, she was a handsome woman, though unlike the girl in coloring.

"My daughter will be pleased. She was quite worried about you." He nodded, the movement making him cringe. "Keep still. You've had a time of it since she brought you here."

Clearing his throat, he rasped, "Who are you?"

The woman smiled. "I am Riona of the Heath, and that is my daughter, Fiadh. You are on Lord Darragh of Felmore's land in Dorcha Wood." Gideon stiffened, recalling the forest's name as one of the last elven strongholds during his grandfather's time. It was said to be a haunted, evil place.

"I am Gideon, son of Lord Ross Hughes of Belfirth."

Riona looked him over, unsurprised to hear he was a noble's son. His clothing alone had hinted as much. "How did you come to our land, stranger?"

"I don't know. My mind… I can't seem to clear it."

Their voices woke the woman by his side, and she slowly came awake, mouth gaping when she saw he was watching her. "You live!" she gushed, turning red at the announcement. "I mean to say, good morrow." Heat crept into her face as she realized she'd been resting on his shoulder, likely drooling and snoring.

He cracked a small smile, though it was strained with fatigue. She had mesmerizing eyes, and he felt lost in them for a moment. They were such a bright green, as though they were illuminated from within, producing a dazzling glow unlike any he had beheld. "It must be from your great care," he responded, his deep voice curling around her.

Getting to her knees, she fidgeted for a moment before asking, "May I?"

At his nod, Fiadh leaned over and peeled back his bandages, the nervous trembling in her hands ceasing as she became the healer and checked his wounds visually for putridity. Inhaling deeply, she used her sense of smell to ferret out any infection she couldn't see but found none. Riona handed her the bowl of water and a cloth. "Clean the wounds and dress them."

Gideon rasped, "Fiadh, I am told I owe you thanks."

"There is no need," she said, ducking her head as she

began assessing every wound, cleansing before wrapping the more egregious with a new poultice her mother prepared.

"Aye, there is," Gideon argued, his words ending in a fit of coughing.

"Drink this," Riona said, holding out a cup made from the horn of a bull. Gideon tried sitting up but fell back, his head spinning. Situating herself behind him, Fiadh propped his head as Riona brought the cup to his lips. A sweet mixture of mead and herbs filled his nostrils and coated his tongue. He swallowed, letting out a sigh as the liquid slid down his swollen throat. "That will help with the fever," Riona told him. Looking at her daughter, she added, "Fiadh, fetch some water."

"Thank you," Gideon croaked, tracking Fiadh's movements as she unhooked a ragged shawl from a peg and slung it around her shoulders with practiced ease. Unlatching the door, Fiadh let in a blast of cool air. He sighed, feeling it bathe his heated face before turning his attention back to Riona.

Grabbing a small bucket, Fiadh stepped into the crisp morning and inhaled deeply. Birds trilled, filling the forest with their song, while furry creatures darted about the small clearing outside the door. Not wanting to keep Gideon waiting, she fetched the water, giving scant attention to the critters who came to visit as was their wont. Returning home, Fiadh heard an indistinct murmur of conversation, mainly her mother's voice, that drifted to silence as she opened the door.

Riona stood at the hearth, stirring porridge over the fire. The smell of oats filled the small space, mixing with the scent of herbs and earth. Setting the bucket on a stool,

Fiadh ladled water into a cup and knelt by Gideon's side to help him drink. He looked up at her with thanks and took a long pull of the liquid, sighing in relief after draining the cup.

"Thank you."

Fiadh nodded. "Better?"

"Aye," he said, though fatigue clouded his handsome face, "but, I have never felt such weakness."

"Would you mind if I looked at your eyes?" Fiadh asked, leaning forward and touching his face near his eye. He consented, and she gently pulled back the lid to look at the sclera. It was still yellowed. "Were you ill before the attack?"

"Your mother asked me the same. Do you see something?"

"You have a yellow tint to the whites of your eyes, which could mean illness."

Tapping a large wooden spoon on the edge of the kettle before setting it on the rim, Riona added, "Or it could be that you were poisoned." She looked at Fiadh. "We were discussing this before you returned. Gideon said he doesn't recall being ill prior to going into battle."

"There was a battle? Do you mean the skirmish with Lord Darragh's men?"

"Nay," Gideon replied. "There was a battle. I fought alongside my brother…" His brow wrinkled. "We were outnumbered by…" He made a frustrated noise. "I can't… I can't remember. I don't know what happened to Doran. Or Father."

Fiadh looked up at her mother, confused by the notion of a small war occurring nearby when they had heard nothing of it. Even outcasts of Felmore learned of such things, as there was little to speak of in such a small village. "Who were you fighting?"

Gideon let out a sigh of frustration. "I don't..." he shook his head.

"If you were in battle, did you not have a horse?"

"Aridius," he told her, swinging his eyes about as though he'd find his steed within the small hut. "You didn't see him when you found me?"

"Nay. There was no horse." Fiadh's eyes skittered to the side as she recalled the mounts of the lord's guard. She glanced at her mother.

"I suppose the blood could have scared it off," Riona offered.

Gideon looked unconvinced.

"It matters not," she continued. "We have no shelter for a horse nor feed."

"This is maddening!" Gideon burst out. "I recall almost nothing of what happened before you found me." He made a strangled sound and clutched his head. "There are just fragments of images, but they make no sense."

The women's eyes met; concern echoed in their expressions. Gideon's memory loss wasn't a result of the wounds they treated, and it seemed unlikely an illness would lead to such a malady. But poison was also not a plausible cause. It left them wondering what was going on in Gideon's mind that kept him from remembering recent events.

Riona knelt at Gideon's head. "I am going to check for a wound." Lifting gently, she palpated his skull, feeling for any raised areas that may indicate a blow. Along the right side, toward its base, she felt a large knot, making Gideon wince when she ran her fingers along it. "Were you struck in the head during the recent attack?"

Gideon tried to recall the events of yesterday, but they were fuzzy. "I don't know."

"Whenever it happened, a blow like that could affect the memory."

"That wouldn't cause the yellowing in his eyes," Fiadh remarked.

"True. I do not know the cause of that." Riona looked down at Gideon. "We can give you infusions to rid your body of illness or poison."

"And my memory?"

Riona pursed her lips. "It can take days or weeks or may never return. I have seen it before. You are welcome to remain with us until you are strong enough to move on." Fiadh smirked at Riona's shift in tone regarding the length of Gideon's recuperation under their care, resulting in a scowl from her mother. "I would ask you not to draw attention to yourself. My daughter and I live a simple life and do well to keep ourselves away from many in the village. Or those who find themselves in the wood." She subtly drew his attention to Fiadh, who had begun to fill bowls with porridge, as she said the last, knowing Gideon would understand the deeper meaning.

"I thank you for your care. I will be on my way as soon as I am able. I must go home. My family…" his voice trailed off. "Something happened. I know it. There was a battle… Doran…" He let out a loud sigh. "I can't remember."

"I find it is best not to force the mind to recall what it isn't ready to," Riona told him, reaching for the bowl Fiadh held out. "Your wounds were deep, and your body still feverish. Eat and rest."

Rolling up her pallet again to use as a support, Fiadh wedged it beneath Gideon's shoulders as he leaned forward, the action causing beads of sweat to pebble his forehead. "I'm weak as a babe."

He may feel weak as one, Fiadh reflected, but he looked nothing like a helpless child. "Do you need help to eat?"

Gideon looked at Fiadh's face, expecting to see pity or irritation at having to help a grown man of a score and three, but saw only openness and innocence that felt at odds with the world he thought he knew. Of course, some of what he knew appeared to have gone the way of the birds in winter, but she was nonetheless intriguing. Holding out a hand that twitched with small tremors, he said, "I can manage."

After they had broken their fast, Riona gathered small clay pots, placing them in a basket before leaving for the village. She would trade her remedies for grain and meat from a small farm on the edge of Felmore that had become somewhat of a trading post for her. Ohran, an elderly farmer and widower whose wife had been nursed for weeks by Riona when she had come down with a sickness of the lungs, had become Riona's trusted link to village life. It was not that others didn't know she visited. They did and left various goods to trade for the salves and infusions Riona crafted. But venturing within the heart of the village as though she were one of them had long since become a thing of the past. Lord Darragh had already taken her husband and son, and Riona feared for Fiadh's safety should she be spotted. So, she kept to the periphery, making infrequent trips to Ohran's farmstead to trade and catch up on village gossip or, on rare occasions, taking up the role of midwife when there was a dire need or specific request.

Following her mother's departure, Fiadh collected eggs from the tiny coop abutting their hut before heading into the woods to gather plants, nuts, and berries for infusions and food stores.

Gideon fell into a deep sleep, images of the chaos of battle, the ring of swords, and screams of men, creating a horrendous landscape. He ran in this dreamworld, legs slogging through mud and gore, chest aching with a frantic effort to reach his brother, Doran.

Gideon never saw what felled him, even in this strange dreamlike state, only watched as though outside himself, as his body hit to the ground, face planted in the trampled earth. Feet, bound in strange wrappings and laced up long calves, stomped past his prone form while alien battle cries sang across the wind as his men hit the ground in muffled thumps all around him. They were surrounded, overpowered from every direction. It was a slaughter. Unable to rise, he watched in dawning horror as every member of his army was skewered upon curved, wickedly sharp blades wielded by men who swung them with unparalleled skill and ease, their exotic faces stamped in dispassionate masks. Gideon was wrenched awake, the sounds of his brother's death scream echoing as the enemy engulfed him.

CHAPTER FIVE

*L*ord Darragh dragged the gangly youth across the putrid rushes covering the great hall's rough stones, his narrow feet digging ruts into moldy masses of rotted hay and leavings from a month's worth of meals. Yanking the lad upright, Darragh spat an accusation in the boy's face. "You dare steal my guardsman's horse!"

The child's teeth clacked loudly, biting into the side of his tongue as his head was thrown back in Darragh's fist. Bloody drool leaked from his mouth as the boy pleaded, "Nay! I found it!"

"Liar!" Darragh thundered, tossing the boy to the ground in a heap. "Where are my men?"

The youngster scuttled a short distance away, his hand sinking into something sticky beneath the fibers coating the floor. "I did not see them, my lord, only the horse. I swear it!"

Darragh paced, his lank blond hair falling in oily clumps around a face that was permanently twisted with cruelty. Reining in his anger, he walked in slow circles, hands flexing in the air rather than around a thin neck. Dark eyes, such a deep brown they looked almost black, bore into the frightened child as he stopped moving and took a deep breath, letting it out in a slow gush to cool his temper. "Found it? You claim you found the mount?" The boy nodded, his body trembling. "What is your name?"

"Tadgh," he whispered, eyeing the soldiers who melted into the room from the shadows.

"Where did you *find* Jarvis' horse, Tadgh?" Darragh crooned, moving closer, so he towered over the boy.

Darting a frightened glance at the men who had formed a loose circle around them, Tadgh gulped, "At the edge of the eastern meadow, just beyond Dorcha Wood."

Mutters and shifting feet followed this pronouncement. "Silence!" Darragh yelled, his piercing stare sweeping the assemblage with disgust. Zeroing in on the boy again, he hissed, "And why did you not bring the horse to *me*?"

"I… I didn't know… who it belon—"

In a blur of movement, Darragh's hand swept across Tadgh's face, the force hurling the boy's body to the side. "You didn't *know*?" he snarled. "You're little more than a thief, and I have no patience for thieves."

Giving Tadgh a vicious kick, Darragh stalked away from the child's whimpering form and toward his men, who stood ready and waiting. "The thief claims he found the mount outside Dorcha Wood, and that is where you will look." His men grumbled, and Darragh's face flooded with anger. "Are you a pack of superstitious women afraid of a few trees?" Those who had quietly groused looked away as Darragh continued, "Sweep the meadow. I want them found. And the Great Mother help you if you think to betray me."

One by one, the men left, conferring with the captain of the guard who doled out instructions under the Darragh's watchful eye. Tadgh, seeing an opportunity to flee, rose slowly, his head pounding, heart racing. Darragh let him get across the hall before he called the hounds and commanded them to circle the lad with snarls and snaps of their massive jaws.

Barking an order, the dogs herded the boy and followed Darragh as he made his way to the dungeon. The frightened breaths of the youth, mixed with low growls of beasts who wanted nothing more than to hear the order to attack, bounced off the walls in strange echoes. Carrying a torch in his hand, Darragh led them into the depths, descending into darkness so thick it swallowed the light. Rarely did he fill the cells of this pit. It was no secret he saw no logic in keeping someone fed and nourished as they underwent interrogations. Darragh's temper was like a living thing, swift and brutal.

No one followed their progress as they reached the bottom of the steps and traveled along dank corridors to a hidden door. With a signal, the hounds halted, keeping Tadgh pinned to the adjacent wall. Unlocking the door with a heavy key, Darragh swung it open, the light from within bathing his sharply pointed face in a ghostly sheen. Sealing himself in with a heavy thunk, he turned to one of the two living things in the room and said, "Mother, I seek your counsel."

The woman, hunched and grey, sat rocking before a small fire whose smoke drifted up a tiny chimney in the top of the outer wall. Strewn about the furnished space was an odd assortment of bones, herbs, and jars of substances better left alone. Her servant, an aging spinster with scraggly hair and missing teeth, bowed low to Darragh and left the room, keeping her back to the door in a show of respect far above the lord's station. He needn't worry about the servant's wagging tongue, having cut it out when he consigned her to his mother's cell. Pulling a chair from beneath a table strewn with bits of food and parchment with unusual markings, Darragh sat before Haegna, the lady of Felmore.

Canting her head, she looked up at him through cloudy blue eyes set in a face with creases so deep years of dirt had become trapped within their folds. "See how you chase away my sweet, Emer." Cackling as she took in his expression, Haegna added, "You've got bloodlust in your eyes, Darragh. Been befouling the Felmore folk with your temper today?"

Darragh grimaced, leaning away as a waft of foul breath from her rotted teeth hit him. "Charming as ever, Mother."

She laughed again, the sound dark and wet. "What brings you?"

"Three of my men have gone missing."

"And you wish to know their whereabouts?" Haegna asked, gripping the arms of her rocker to stand.

Dredging up a pretense of chivalry, Darragh took her frail arm, feeling the brittle bones beneath his fingers and imagining clenching his hand so tightly they broke. Her dress, once fashionable, was now as fragile as she was, thin and worn, so easy to rip to pieces like her flesh, should he give in to the desire that prowled his mind.

Dropping her too roughly onto the chair before a pedestal, on top of which sat a wide bowl of dark liquid, Haegna snapped at him, "Mind yourself, you careless runt!"

Darragh ground his teeth, hate spilling from him in palpable waves. She saw it and snickered.

Settling her withered frame more fully, she looked up, reaching out a hand and stroking his face. "Ah, my sweet boy, I do so love your visits," Haegna crooned and leaned forward; her face mirrored on the still substance of the bowl.

To the people of Felmore, Haegna was long dead, having drawn her last breath a few years after the passing of her husband, Lorcan. It was Darragh who consigned her to darkness, keeping her hidden as her madness grew. But his mercy wasn't born of love. Rather, he had always been drawn to darkness. Even as a child, whether it was in his heart or the world around him. Darragh fed on it like a glutton.

Haegna was an embodiment of that malevolence. Her inherent cruelty had been the example for a youth whose father had disregarded the frail child of his loins, leaving young Darragh to cling to a woman who molded him like clay. A warped aberration who had grown into a man of power. The people of Felmore were his playthings, toys to hone his skill and feed his deviant hunger. A hunger that was never satiated.

CHAPTER SIX

The madness had always lived within Haegna. However, when Darragh was a child it had been tightly reined by his father, until the man took his last breath after a lengthy and dreadful illness. Lorcan's death had loosed a mania within his mother to escape such a fate. Haegna started dabbling in dark arts, witchcraft so demonic Darragh could only wonder how she had come upon such knowledge. Her mind broke, and she fed on those around her like a succubus. The first time he discovered his mother drinking the blood of a hapless servant girl, he had been both repulsed and fascinated. She had claimed, as he stood raging at her, that consuming the blood of youth would infuse her with vitality, keeping the crows of death from circling. As years passed and more children from among the servants went missing, people whispered of dark magic, seeing the castle and its inhabitants as devils.

But her lust for blood and youthfulness knew no boundaries, and there came a time when she sought from without those stone walls.

"Fetch me a youth from the village," she had purred as Darragh sat with her in the solar.

He sighed. "The people will talk if I take one from within the village. We have spoken of this."

"Aye, we have spoken of it, but that was before. Emer has told me of a boy the villagers whisper of. He has green eyes, and is… unusual. You will find him and bring him to me."

"I will do no such thing."

"Do it for me, my son. Do it for your mother… who loves you." Haegna leaned in close to Darragh, kissing his cheek and neck, until he swatted her away, earning him a girlish giggle.

He glared at her. "Your words do not sway me."

"Then do it for yourself," she told him, settling back in her chair.

His ears perked. "Explain your meaning."

"This boy, if what the peasants say is true, could have powers even you could harvest."

"Powers? What powers?" Darragh asked.

"They say he brought a bird back from the dead."

Darragh scoffed. "You've been fooled, Mother."

"Perhaps, but what if the story is true? Those who saw it tell how the bird had broken its neck and lay dead. The boy picked it up, cradling it in his hands, before tucking it against his chest for a time. When he opened his fingers, it flew away, uninjured. Imagine what his blood could do for me… for you?"

Looking away from Haegna's eager face, he considered her words. When she had begun this foul obsession with consuming the blood of youths, he had placated her, played along. He would tell her that, aye, age had been beaten back, that it had receded from her visage and been replaced with vitality. But, he admitted, there had been times when it wasn't pretense. It made him wonder at the possibilities of what she proposed.

"Mayhap," she continued, "he is some blood relation to the Aos Sí. Think what we could do if *their* magic lives in him."

The bait was seized and swallowed. Darragh set out to find the child, coming across him and his father as they went to market to sell wool from their tiny sheep farm on the edge of the village. The man had tried to fight him off but had no skill with a blade and was quickly dispatched, with a quick thrust of Darragh's sword. The boy, unusual with his vibrant green eyes and fair skin, had bit and scratched as birds swooped and screeched while they tussled, their talons finding the flesh on Darragh's head and neck. The burst of chaos ended abruptly when he struck the child into unconsciousness, leaving the crows and hawks shrieking in their flight back toward the forest.

They had almost made it to the castle when a strange bank of clouds rolled in from Dorcha Wood, dark and ominous, filling the sky so quickly that it went from day to dusk in moments. The wind howled, whipping up leaves and loose articles of clothing that had been hung to dry, pulling them into the air in tiny funnels. The horses spooked, tossing their heads and stamping until their riders cuffed them into silence. And then the sky erupted. Bolts of lightning arced across the horizon in thunderous claps. A giant oak, easily hundreds of years old, was struck by a bolt so violent the air sizzled. It fell with a weighty crash, crushing the three men who rode before Darragh and his captive. His horse reared, throwing the two of them to the ground where Darragh's head found a rock, and all went black. When he woke, the boy was nowhere to be found. Only animal tracks remained where his body must have landed, telling their version of his fate. Darragh had raged at the loss, growing furious when he discovered the farmer's wife and daughter had fled.

Haegna was incensed upon finding out, demanding he locate the boy's sister, but it was for naught. The woman and her child had disappeared, and none within the village knew of their whereabouts. Darragh let her rant for days until she exhausted herself. Eventually, she returned to her practice of preying on servants while word of her evil spread to every home in Felmore. Darragh had relished the fear his mother had inspired, believing he could control her, being the one who provided her with the victims who fed her deviant appetite. Sometimes, he would even watch, his blood heating at the sights and sounds that filled her chambers. But those feelings didn't outlast the murder of his betrothed.

Haegna had been welcoming, lavishing compliments on his young bride as she moved into the halls of Felmore. The girl was a good match, being the niece of Lord Crommack, a powerful man whose alliance could pave the way toward his ambition to control the western reaches. Darragh had watched the interactions with indifference, letting his mother play her part. He knew what she was and found it laughable that the ruse was so successful. Darragh had assumed that, despite her madness, she still possessed some modicum of wit, enough sense to limit her perversions to the servants, prisoners, and those few lowborn youths and maidens from the village he occasionally brought her way. It had been folly to assume such. His indifference turned to disgust when he came upon Haegna bathing, having been summoned by Emer, whose cries for help had sent him rushing up the steps to his mother's chamber. Somehow, Haegna had managed to suspend the corpse of his butchered wife above the copper bathing tub and lay sprawled under her hanging body as blood dripped from a dozen stab wounds throughout her torso. She cackled as Darragh burst into the chamber, smearing blood on her face and arms, her hair matted with it.

"What have you done?" Darragh had thundered, stalking toward her.

"I have rid you of your puling wife and bathed in her vitality. See how the shadow of death has left me," she smiled, her teeth stark white beneath the gore.

Darragh growled and reached for the ropes that bound the body of his wife, cutting them ruthlessly while Emer stood sobbing in the corner. "Silence!" he roared, eliciting giggles from Haegna, who licked her fingers. "You have gone too far, Mother," Darragh snarled. "Emer, fetch a basin of water and clean her up."

Hoisting the corpse from the room, he tossed it on the bed, not caring about soiling the sheets. He couldn't allow this to get out. The villagers would drag her from the castle and burn her at the stake. Lord Crommack would raise his banners and have a thousand men storming Felmore Castle. Pacing, Darragh muttered, finally pulling his dagger from its sheath and stalked toward Haegna, who still sat in the tub. She watched him come, her face a macabre mask of insanity. Tilting her head back to expose her neck, she goaded him, cackling when he faltered. He couldn't do it. Not her. At that moment, Darragh decided to fake his mother's death and tucked her away in the darkness.

Over time, the madness which consumed Haegna became a lure Darragh could not resist. Dark. Forbidden. Rabid. Filled with visions and prophecies, whether real or imagined, it mattered little in the face of their violence. He wanted them to come to fruition, needing them in the way a man seeks release with a woman. Only Darragh's need was a thirst so powerful he cast reason aside, putting faith in a woman whose mind was a fractured, ugly thing.

CHAPTER SEVEN

*N*ow, Darragh kept Haegna tucked away, the mute Emer her sole company and caretaker, visiting when it served a purpose. And always with the promise of a gift.

"My men have gone missing," he reminded her as she looked into the liquid. "I want to know where they are."

"Aye," she tsked. "Men abandoning their lord are tidings of misfortune. Have you a gift to wet my parched tongue?"

Darragh grimaced. "After you have told me what I have come for, you will get your reward."

Smiling, Haegna brushed aside strands of grey hair and looked into the dark pool, her milky eyes like phantoms staring back at her. She muttered, the clarity of the sounds growing fuzzy as bizarre phrases pooled on the surface of the liquid. Ripples crawled slowly to the edges of the bowl and back to the center in a hypnotic rhythm. Minutes passed as he sat mesmerized by his mother's invocations, at war with the parts of himself that were both covetous of her power and repelled by it. Darragh saw the moment Haegna found what she sought, a smug look crossing her face as her shoulders drooped with exhaustion. She sat back, her arms dropping limply at her sides, looking older, more haggard.

Swiveling her face to her son, she laughed, the sound bouncing off the walls, through the floor, and up his spine, until they echoed in his mind, filling him with a flare of anger so fierce, he lunged, grabbing her throat. "You dare mock me!"

She choked, but the merriment remained, stamped on her face, daring him to squeeze, as she gasped and turned purple. Darragh snarled, his brown teeth like fangs in a face filled with malice. Ripping his hands away, he lurched from his chair, grabbing his head. "You drive me to madness, witch! I should kill you and free the world of your evil."

"Then do it," Haegna entreated, "my life is nearly spent as it is. What matter if you end it sooner? Of course," she said slyly, "you will never know what I have seen if you kill me now."

"Tell me," he snarled, saliva spraying from his mouth.

"I did not find your men. They have gone where I can't see them. Some power keeps their whereabouts from me. Whether they are dead or alive, I cannot say."

"Then what good are you?"

Haegna eyed her son, noting his gaunt features, the cruelty etched within them, so easy to see even for those who had no sight. "I know of one who could help you, though his kind is not so easy to find. Or catch." Her eyes canted toward the door, and she cocked her head as the sound of Tadgh whimpering in fear reached her ears. "I hear my present just beyond that door. You are too good to me," she said, licking her pale lips.

Darragh pursed his lips. "You'll get nothing if you don't tell me of whom you speak."

She pouted for a moment. "Xander."

"I know of no man by that name," Darragh said, his frustration growing. "Why should I seek him out?"

"He is a mage."

He raised his brows. A mage? Long ago, during the Great War, mages fought beside the Aos Sí, allied with the elven race until they were enticed by a power far greater than the elves. It was said the mages banded together, aligning themselves with a dark being whose origins remained unknown to this day. The mages turned on the Aos Sí, slaughtering countless, before the elves mustered their strength and struck back, sending those who survived into exile. Years had gone by with nary a whisper of their existence, only frightening stories of their power and evil remaining.

If they were so powerful, Darragh thought, then how is it that men, with naught but steel and bow, could out-fight both them and their little elven friends combined? "No one has seen a mage for decades," he said dismissively.

"Aye," Haegna countered, watching with narrowed eyes as her son walked toward the door shaking his head and muttering.

"And yet…" he paused when her voice carried across the room, scratching at his mind. She smiled, enjoying the game. "There is one ripe for the taking, and should you capture him, he will tell you of your men. And your future."

CHAPTER EIGHT

Gideon looked unwell when Fiadh returned bearing a basket laden with provisions. His face had an unhealthy sheen, pale and sickly with a yellow tinge like the whites of his eyes. She felt him look at her, the pull of his stare like a string tugging her toward him, though she was self-conscious in his presence. Setting aside the basket, she crouched next to Gideon in the dimness of the hut and timidly laid her wrist on his forehead. His skin felt warm but not hot. The fever had abated. But he seemed worse off than when she and her mother had left.

"How do you feel?" she asked, wincing at how loud her voice sounded in the quiet.

Gideon swallowed, the lump in his throat bobbing. "Awful."

Worry suffused her face, bringing the healer within to the surface. "Did you sleep?" she asked, running her fingers along his neck to feel his pulse. It was strong, though fast for someone who had been lying about.

"I did, but my dreams…" he told her, shaking his head,

"I can't remember details, but there were screams of men, Doran among them."

"Doran? You called his name when you were with fever."

"My brother."

She nodded, glancing away for a moment. *I had a brother once*, she thought, though her memories of him were hazy things time had worn away. Still, Fiadh sometimes felt him in her thoughts as though a piece of him had been left behind inside of her. "Were you with him before you were attacked outside the wood?"

"I believe so," he started. "I must have been, but I can't be sure. There is something at the edge of my mind, and I can't hold on to it. I can't remember the events before you found me. Of my home and childhood, I have perfect clarity, but anything beyond the festivities of Malbon is garbled or gone altogether."

Malbon had been a sennight ago, which left a significant amount of time unaccounted for. "Time can heal wounds. Perhaps the loss of your memories will be among them." Selecting various herbs from the rafters, Fiadh began grinding them into a fine powder, mixing them with lichen she had picked that morning. She poured the concoction into a cup of weak mead. "Drink this. It will help purge your body of impurities." She watched him drink it down, smiling at his grimace when he got to the dregs, which she knew from experience to be bitter.

"Thank you, Fiadh," he said, settling back as his eyes began to close.

She liked the sound of her name on his lips, unused to hearing anyone utter it, aside from Mother. It had been years since she had spoken to another soul. That lack of interaction suddenly felt oppressive. Fiadh made a face and wandered out the door, leaving Gideon resting as the herbs took effect. In his presence, she caught a glimpse of something that had been kept out of reach, something alluring, and now she wanted it with renewed desire.

Over time, Fiadh had become more myth than flesh to the people of Felmore. They whispered of the lady of the forest who would appear just inside the border of Dorcha Wood, animals at her side, only to vanish like mist. Some claimed she was no spirit at all, only the daughter of Riona, the wilding woman who'd gone mad with grief after her husband and son's deaths and fled into the forest. All knew Riona was real enough, of course, and that she visited the village from time to time, but most avoided her when she did unless they had need of her herbs or potions. But seldom had known of Fiadh, and her legend grew and spread through the village. It had pleased Riona to hear such things as she visited Ohran's farmstead. She had done nothing to dissuade the rumors, not admitting Fiadh lived and thankful that most of the villagers resented Darragh, never revealing, as years had passed, that she still resided within reach of his fiefdom. His evil and indifference had become protection as her daughter had gone from real to imagined.

Now, Fiadh's only companions were those who didn't wear a human face, whose bodies and minds were as wild as the forest they dwelled in. But Fiadh longed to interact with others, at times finding herself roaming the outskirts of Felmore, hoping to catch a glimpse of someone her age and wondering if she could defy her mother wholly and step into that forbidden world. She almost did a few times, but Mother's warnings always stayed her feet, anchoring her under the safety of the trees. Occasionally, she felt it was more than Riona's words that kept her hidden, as though some mysterious force played a part, there in the whispers of the trees or the voices in the wind.

Most days, Fiadh tolerated Mother's rules with grim acceptance, but there were times when sparks of rebellion flared, and she ran through the woods, wild things in flight and on foot at her side, wanting nothing more than to be free to come and go as she saw fit, and with whom she wished. Riona's worries be damned.

Gideon slipped in and out of a healing sleep as the day wore on, under the watchful care of Fiadh, and with each passing hour, he brightened up, healthy color returning to his face and lightness to his features. With her aid, Gideon sat and chatted for periods of time, though she rarely knew what to say, averting her eyes as awkward pauses made conversation stilted. He didn't appear to notice, which put her at ease.

By the time Riona walked through the doorway with the shadows of late afternoon blanketing the woods, he had consumed another infusion, a small helping of vegetable stirabout, and was sitting up, his back resting against the wall.

Putting her basket down, Riona greeted her daughter and then crouched at Gideon's side. "May I look at your eyes?" He nodded. Peeling back an eyelid, she asked Fiadh, "Have you given him infusions?"

"Aye, two and food at midday."

"Good," Riona said, observing both sclerae. "And have you passed waters?" she asked him, causing Gideon to redden.

"Aye."

"Rest, and the drafts my daughter gave you, have begun to leech the toxins from your body. Already, I can see an improvement in your color."

"She has healing ways," Gideon commented, casting a glance at Fiadh.

"More than you know," Riona said so softly he almost missed it.

The day wore on and evening descended, the hours peppered by children's stories Gideon had heard throughout his formative years, tall tales of sprites whose antics wrought havoc throughout village life brought smiles and laughter to the women. They were fictions Mother had never spoken, and they felt like the forbidden tales they were, outlawed by Darragh, which made the telling of them more enticing.

"Let me tell you a tale of the gruagach," Gideon said.

"The what?" Fiadh asked, looking at her mother, who rolled her eyes.

"You've not heard of the little folk?"

Fiadh nodded. "Oh, aye, I have heard of them, just not by that name."

"Well, we had, like all houses, a family of gruagach who lived in our kitchen," he said with a wink. "They are shy folk, you see, never wanting to show themselves. Always hiding in dark corners and unused crevices. But Doran and I knew they were about."

Fiadh smiled and settled onto her pallet. Hearing a story reminded her of her younger years when her mother's voice would spin fanciful worlds through her head as she fell asleep.

"Gruagach, by their nature, are helpful folk, often doing small chores in the wee hours when the household sleeps. This made it challenging for Doran and me to catch one, as we could never seem to stay awake. But one day, we made plans and somehow managed to keep our eyes open. Now, the gruagach are given gifts by the kitchen maid. Else they would leave the house. So, Doran and I decided we would use a comb of honey we had fetched earlier that day and place it on the small offering stone in a dark corner of the kitchen. When the gruagach showed itself to collect its gift, we would capture it in a basket!"

The women laughed at the picture his words painted.

"All was going as planned. Cook rested, his huge form snoring in a small room off the kitchen, and no one was about. Sneaking inside that forbidden place." Gideon paused and looked at them. "I should probably tell you cook had banned us from the kitchen some months before. But that is another story," he said with a grin. "We crept to the offering stone and set the honeycomb upon it, then hid in a nook a few paces away. Doran and I waited for what seemed like hours but was likely only one. I don't know who fell asleep first, but it was to cook swatting us with a broom that we awoke. We never did see or catch a gruagach, but the honeycomb was gone by morning."

Fiadh clapped, her face alight with humor. Gideon was an entrancing storyteller. Hearing him meld his childhood adventures to a story of a fantastical creature caused her to begin to see him as the man he was beneath the brutal soldier she had witnessed. When he started a tale of the sluagh, Riona cut him off, earning a grumble from Fiadh, which turned into a gulp as Riona shot her a stern warning.

"Gideon must rest if he is to recover, Fiadh," she scolded.

"Aye, Mother."

"I will regale you with more stories on the morrow," Gideon promised, earning him a shy smile.

Riona watched her daughter interact with Gideon and realized the cost of hiding her away. She was a grown woman, ripe for marriage, yet she had never spoken to a man. It filled her with guilt to see how strained Fiadh was around him, though she knew there had never been a choice. Riona had known that if they had stayed in Felmore, Darragh would have come for Fiadh, and she would have been powerless to stop him. But... she could have taken Fiadh far from here, to another town where no one knew them. Instead, she had chosen to stay, too filled with grief to do more than muster the strength to abandon their tiny farm and hide in the woods. *Would life have been better for her if I had made a different choice?* Riona wondered. The thought churned in her mind until she realized that it didn't matter what village they lived in. People would've noted how unusual Fiadh was, and that realization was dangerous. *They never would've let me take her from Dorcha Wood,* a little voice added.

At least now, she was safe, and perhaps... perhaps Gideon would be a path to a different future, one in which her daughter would be surrounded by people who loved her. Riona smiled softly, thinking of how much she would miss her daughter if that came to pass while also wanting so much more for her than the small world she knew. Of course, there was the genuine possibility Fiadh could never leave Dorcha Wood, that it had claimed her. *She was never really mine*, Riona acknowledged, remembering that day in the woods when her life had changed forever, when a woman, unlike any she had known, had crossed her path and set her on a new course.

She looked at her daughter as Fiadh fussed about and tidied the single-room home for longer than was necessary, finally settling in with a contented sigh. Riona doused the lamp, bathing the room in darkness. Someday, she would tell Fiadh everything. She had to. The world was closing in on them. Gideon's arrival proved that, and Riona worried there would come a day when it came crashing into their lives, like a wild bull. If that happened, Fiadh needed to know. She must understand who she really was. Turning toward the wall, Riona calmed her mind and let sleep come.

A few paces away, Fiadh settled in and listened to Gideon. His breathing rapidly took on a deep quality of sleep, as her mind relived the images conjured by his voice. Where did those stories come from? Was there any truth to them, or were they merely spun by those whose minds were far more creative than hers?

"Little people," she scoffed, muttering softly in the quiet. If tiny humans were wandering the village of Felmore, she would have learned of it long before now. Shaking her head, Fiadh curled onto her side, bunching up the edge of her pallet under her cheek. Calling out a soft goodnight to her mother and receiving a hushed reply, she closed her eyes.

CHAPTER NINE

The next day, Riona forced Gideon up and about with a sturdy walking stick, insisting he use his muscles rather than let them grow weak. It was laborious work, but he admitted after the second day that he felt stronger.

"My manor would benefit from your skills," he told her as they took a short stroll around the small clearing in front of the hut.

Riona snorted. "I would wager you have healers aplenty, and if your people are anything like many of Felmore, they may not welcome someone with my skills."

Assessing her, Gideon countered, "I wouldn't think such a thing would stop you."

"Perhaps, you're right," she chuckled, "but my daughter and I will not leave these woods. This is our home."

"The offer remains."

Riona smiled, leading him inside, where she gathered ointments and infusions for a trek to the village. Fiadh was surprised to see her mother readying herself for another trip to Felmore. "You are returning to the village so soon?"

"Aye," she said, acknowledging the unusual nature of a repeated visit. "We have no fresh beef bones, and Gideon needs a bone marrow broth to build up his strength. I asked Ohran to send word to the butcher." Fiadh and her mother rarely ate meat, the idea of consuming the flesh of animals was repellent to Fiadh when she could feel them in her mind, and Riona was respectful of her squeamishness.

Riona finished packing her basket, giving Fiadh a few instructions before she left, and headed out, leaving her daughter with the task of pushing Gideon to be up and about. After the noon meal, she and Gideon took a stroll.

"You are a fine healer, Fiadh," he said, his voice rich, though tinged with weariness.

"Thank you," she said shyly. "I have learned at Mother's hand since I was a child. It is she who is the true healer. I am yet an apprentice."

"Do not discount your talents. Yours is a tender hand and heart, and I am the better for it." His legs trembled, but he forced himself to walk, nudging the hand she stretched to aid him aside. "I must do this."

"As you will," Fiadh said, walking a short distance away to where a small rabbit sat waiting, under cover of a scraggly bush. She sat, and Gideon watched as the creature crept to her side, keeping a wary eye on him until she reached down and stroked its velvety fur.

"His pelt would make a fine lining for a pair of gloves," Gideon said and jerked his head to the hare.

Fiadh gave him a look of disgust. "I would never kill Saebal for his fur!"

Gideon arched his brow. "You have named him?"

"Aye, and what of it?"

He shook his head and looked down before casting his eyes at her with a smirk.

"You wretch!" she yelled, her natural timidity falling away as though something had clicked into place in her mind. "You were jesting!"

"Aye, but it was worth the fire from your tongue," Gideon chuckled. "And I would hear more of it," he added, waggling his eyebrows. Fiadh blushed, looking flustered. He enjoyed her reaction for a moment before asking, "Would you fetch my sword?" Fiadh gasped. "Not for the hare!" he said, throwing his hands up. "I must practice."

Fiadh patted Saebal on his rump and sent him off. The sword felt heavy in her grip as she pulled it from behind a stool. The haft was smooth and unadorned, meant for battle, not beauty. Along the blade, she saw evidence of innumerable encounters in the knicks and scrapes that marred the surface. Fiadh stepped outside and handed the weapon to Gideon, watching as his fingers curled around it with intense familiarity. He spun the blade in his hand, and it cut through the air with a soft whistle. Finding a spot on a fallen log she and her mother used as a bench, Fiadh sat and watched Gideon work. The sword glinted as sunlight filtering through the clearing hit the blade. She stared in awe at his skill, though it was true she had little to compare it to. He worked in practiced rhythms, focused on nothing but the arcs and swings of his tool of war until his arms trembled from the strain. Stabbing it into the ground, Gideon leaned forward, hands pressed to his upper thighs, taking huge pulls of breath as beads of sweat ran down his face in tiny rivulets.

"I think," he panted, "that is enough for today. Help me inside, would you?"

Fiadh trotted to him, slung his arm over her shoulder, and tugged the sword from the earth, rocking backward slightly when it finally pulled free. "You are a great swordsman."

"Aye?"

She nodded.

"And how many swordsmen have you seen?"

Fiadh bit her lip. "One?"

Gideon laughed. "Well, I appreciate your compliment, regardless. Now, take me to my pallet before I embarrass myself and fall on my face."

Fiadh met Riona outside when she made her way through a small break in the trees hours later. Taking in the empty basket, Fiadh frowned. "Were you paid in coin, then?"

Sighing, Riona shook her head. "The butcher had no fresh bones to spare. The blight has spoiled the crops and starved his cattle. It is worse this year, and countless are suffering, though Lord Darragh has yet to shell out any coin to purchase grain for the townsfolk. Many are getting sick. It is a blessing to live outside those misfortunes, though I grieve for them."

Fiadh had forgotten about the blight. It was a hardship she felt sorrow for, though its effects had little impact on their day-to-day. Such was the cycle of life, from what she had discerned. There had been famine and plague over the years that had, at times, kept Riona from venturing into the village. This year, to hear it was worse made Fiadh wonder what her life would have been like had she and her mother remained in Felmore. Would they have survived such privation? Taking the basket and her mother's shawl, Fiadh briefly reviewed their patient's progress.

Patting Fiadh's cheek with motherly affection, Riona told her, "One day, your skill will surpass my own."

"I doubt that." Fiadh leaned in, giving her mother a gentle hug. "Do you bring any news? Was there talk of the attack on Gideon?"

Riona's brow creased. "It was quite strange. Ohran said Lord Darragh's guards were searching for three men who had gone missing but found no sign of them. I find it odd that they didn't come across the bodies. Of course, if they had, we could find ourselves in a bad way."

Fiadh averted her gaze, thinking of the Cù-Sìth, but said nothing. "Let us hope they don't find those men. The village is better off without them, anyway."

"It is not for us to decide the fate of men, Fiadh," Riona chided. "That power rests with our Great Mother."

Fiadh nodded.

Brushing off her hands, Riona checked on Gideon, who sat quietly on one of the stools, watching their dialogue. "The yellow of your eyes has all but gone," she pronounced.

"I can feel my strength returning under the care of you both. In two day's time, I shall return to my home and hope the journey restores my memory."

Riona nodded. "You should be strong enough by then. Now, I must collect my supplies." She cast about for what she needed, tucking various items into the basket that had been set aside earlier.

"You cannot mean to leave again!" Fiadh shouted. "How often have you said visits to Felmore are a risk? How often have you told me to keep hidden and not be seen by the townsfolk? And now you visit a third time in mere days!"

"Fiadh, don't raise your voice to me," Riona admonished. "You know these are unusual circumstances. It was you who brought a man in need of aid into our home, and because you did, we must care for him."

Fiadh huffed. "And you leave now, as evening approaches, to *trade* for goods to help him?"

Riona set down the familiar tools she held in her hand and looked at Fiadh. "Iona, the tanner's wife, is in labor. It is her first, and her good husband, Dugan, came to Ohran's home to ask me to attend her."

The fit of outrage left her in a gush. It wasn't fair of her to lash out at Mother. "I'm sorry."

Riona cupped Fiadh's cheek. "I know you chafe at my rules, daughter, but I set them before you to protect you, not keep you captive." Fiadh nodded. "Help me gather my birthing supplies." Fiadh, familiar with her mother's needs, helped Riona gather what she required through what would likely be long hours throughout the night. "Shall I come with you?"

"Nay, daughter. Remain here with Lord Hughes."

It was strange to hear Riona refer to him by his title. He seemed an ordinary man rather than one of nobility. But then, Fiadh had never interacted with those whose station was so far above her own. She hadn't interacted with anyone. Gideon interrupted her thoughts, "Call me Gideon. My father is Lord."

"As you wish," Riona replied with a smile of approval. "I am off to see to the tanner's wife." The women embraced briefly, and Riona left, latching the door behind her.

CHAPTER TEN

By mid-morning, Riona hadn't returned. While it was not unheard of for women to experience long hours of labor, Fiadh sensed something was wrong. After making an infusion for Gideon, she set aside a small meal for the noon hour should he get hungry and grabbed her shawl, preparing to venture to the village.

Gideon eyed her preparations, limping to a stool that sat by the hearth. "Should you be leaving?"

Wrapping the shawl tightly against her body, she looked at him. "Mother may need my help. It must be a difficult birth for her to be still gone. Is there anything I can do for you before I go?"

He shook his head, pleased the motion didn't cause pains shooting through his skull. "Your mother would not want you to leave," he told her.

It didn't take much to recognize something must have happened or been overheard, which led to such restrictions on Fiadh's interactions with the townsfolk. As a man, he had only to look at her to feel desire and know there were some who would have no qualms taking what they wanted. He had seen it before on his lands and had meted out punishments alongside his father for those transgressions. But something in what Riona had said led him to believe there was more to her protectiveness than safeguarding her daughter's innocence.

Fiadh smiled, amused at his reluctance to let her leave. Not that he could do anything to stop her in his current state. "Rest while I am gone. I will return as soon as I am able."

"You shouldn't be leaving," he muttered.

"You are not my warden," Fiadh snapped. "You and my mother seem to be under the delusion that I am unable to care for myself. I assure you, that is not the case."

Gideon sighed, stretching out his bad leg with a wince. "I know you are not a child, Fiadh, but your mother is protective for a reason and has walked this earth longer than you. Perhaps you should listen to her wisdom." She made a face, fussing with her shawl to avoid his stare as he continued, "But you are correct, I am not your keeper."

Fiadh looked up, forcing a smile. "Thank you."

He waved her away, tilting the stool to lean his head against the wall. "Mind where you are and who you see, Fiadh. The world holds many evils."

"I will, and I will return with Mother." She closed the door, then popped her head back in, reminding him, "Be sure you take a few turns in the clearing to work your muscles."

"Aye, as you say," he grimaced with annoyance.

Chuckling at his look of consternation, Fiadh latched the door and turned her back to the hut, cocking her head to listen to the sounds of the forest as she took a step into the woods. It was oddly quiet, as though nature was holding her breath. Unsettled by the silence, she looked through the copse of trees before slowly making her way along a hidden path to the village. Fiadh's apprehension increased as she walked in the crisp air, calling softly to the birds and beasts who always came to her hand. Today, they remained absent, though she felt their eyes on her.

She heard the yells long before the break in the trees that separated Dorcha Wood from the hamlet of Felmore. Leaving the path, she skirted the tree line, keeping to the shadows while following the sound of voices raised in anger. Ducking behind a large oak across from the village center, she peered through the season's last orange leaves clinging to a sapling. Townsfolk formed a loose circle, their hands raised in fists of anger, punctuating shouts that rained upon the normally peaceful village. Scanning the crowd, Fiadh looked for her mother, trepidation growing as each face, twisted with anger, failed to reveal Riona. Darting behind another tree, she stood on her toes and stared at the center of a growing number of people.

Blood drained from her face as she saw her mother, her face bloodied as she pleaded with folded hands. "Dugan," Riona cried, her voice gone hoarse, "I understand your grief, but I am not the cause of the death of your wife and son."

Fiadh sucked in a breath, choking out a whispered, "Nay!"

"Lies!" Dugan thundered. "You're an Aos Sí witch! Iona begged for her life as you fed her poisons and worked your evil."

"Murderer!" Someone shouted, causing Riona to spin and find the voice, her face a mask of horror at the accusation.

"Please, you know me," she pleaded to Dugan. "You begged me to tend your wife." Turning her head slowly, Riona spoke to the angry mass. "You all know me. I have given you medicines, tended you when you were ill, brought healthy babes into the world." She paused, surveying faces who now wore masks of blame. "How many of you have I aided? How many have my remedies saved?"

A man stepped forward, his back to Fiadh so she couldn't see his face. "You have tended us, but who is to say you didn't cause the sickness you cured?"

"Nay! I would never!" Riona pleaded.

Dugan stalked toward her, his face so close to her mother's that flecks of spit sprayed into Riona's eyes as he yelled, "You're an elven witch!" before punching her so hard she spun to the side and crumpled onto the ground.

Face twisting in agony, Fiadh let out a whimper from her hiding spot, hands knotting her dress. "Mother," she cried.

Two men swooped forward, grabbing her mother's limp form. Dugan dug his fingers into Riona's chin, tilting her slack face with a rough twist. "We have invited this woman among us," he yelled, "and now we see her for what she truly is—a murderess witch! It is she who has brought the blight on us! She has doomed us all while she hides in that foul forest!"

"Burn her!" The butcher's wife screamed, a chorus of agreement following.

Like most villages, at its heart was a large platform where announcements were made, and public punishments meted out. The pole anchored to the center of the platform was meant to strap a body for lashings, but now the villagers were calling for a darker use of this hateful construct. Chants filled the air as Riona was dragged through the crowd and lashed to the pole. She roused as people threw rocks and rotted food, flinching as pieces struck her face and body.

"Please!" she screamed, her voice a strangled mass of sound, "Do not do this. I am one of you!"

"Aos Sí witch! Murderer! Sorceress!" The townsfolk cried, hurling refuse at her. Rancid meat slapped against her cheek, leaving a brown smear before thumping to the wooden platform with a smack, followed by moldy cabbage thrown with such force Riona's teeth sliced through her lips when it knocked into her mouth. She spat blood, a long line of drool hanging from her bottom lip. Her panicked eyes darted from face to face as insults and accusations, clods of dirt and wasted food, hurled against her in a rain of hysteria. Finally, a large stone struck the side of her head, and she sagged, the weight of her body straining against the rope that bound her. Riona's head, hanging limply, was now a mottled collection of putrid food and blood.

Face twisting in agony, Fiadh let out a sob as she stood rooted, watching a nightmare unfold before her immobile form. "Mother."

Suddenly, the crowd parted as the lord of Felmore entered the square, a small contingent of his guard at his sides. "Silence!" he bellowed. "What is going on here?"

Peasants, serfs, and craftsmen ducked their heads in obedience, clamping their mouths shut. The tanner stepped forward and leveled his damning accusation. "Riona of

Dorcha Wood has killed my wife and son with her elven powers. She is an Aos Sí witch!"

Strolling toward Riona, an ugly sneer on his face, Darragh looked at her closely. "Riona," he whispered, a memory stirring at the name as realization slowly dawned. This was the woman who had vanished from the village when he had killed her husband and taken her son. It galled him to realize she had been under his nose all along, hiding in that cursed forest. And she had had a daughter all those years ago. His mother had begged for the child to wet her tongue, but he had thought she had left with the girl and settled in other parts. It was foolish of her to remain so close at hand. Could the girl have lived? he wondered. It appeared he might need to go hunting after this business was done.

A nasty gleam filled his features as he shouted, "There is no place among us for women who practice the forbidden arts of the Aos Sí! They are a condemned race, eradicated from our kingdom decades ago for their evil sorcery!" Yells of approval rang out. Lord Darragh silenced them with a swing of his hand. "Three of my men have gone missing." His eyes swept the crowd. "I say this woman lured them with her sorcery before committing some foul deed!"

Fiadh shuddered at the reference to the men Gideon had killed. It made her wonder if the lord's guard had even searched for the men, and if asked to enter Dorcha Wood, had run rather than enter the infamous forest.

Darragh pointed at Riona's unconscious form. "I see this woman's hand in their disappearance, as surely as her evil has taken the life of your good wife and the babe she carried."

Dugan dropped his head. "She was a good woman," he sobbed, "never harmed another soul, and this *elf witch*," Dugan snarled, "snuffed out her life as surely as she took the life of my son before he drew his first breath."

Darragh briefly rested his hand on the man's shoulder before addressing the restless crowd. "I have heard tell of this witch of the woods. Her and her deceased spawn. It is said she fornicates with animals and bathes in the blood of newborns she steals from their cribs. She plagues our fields and poisons our wells year after year." Casting a glance through the crowd, gauging the effect of his words, he shouted, "What punishment shall we impose on this vessel of evil? This murdering whore?"

"Kill her!" Rang through the square, followed by chants to burn her at the stake.

Flinging out his arms, Darragh silenced the crowd. "Let this be a lesson to all who witness. Aos Sí witchery will not be abided, and those who practice it shall be put to death!"

Cheers rang out as the guard was sent off to collect wood and kindling for the burning. Tears streamed down Fiadh's cheeks, and she watched in horror as bundles of dried grasses and sticks were set around the block on which her mother stood.

Riona remained still, her body limp against the rope that bound her tightly to the pole. Fiadh could see a long trail of blood from her mother's left temple running down her cheek, soaking into the collar of her woolen dress. She must have lost consciousness with the blow. One of the guardsmen brought a torch from the smithy's and stood just beyond her mother's pyre, awaiting permission to set it alight.

"Before we condemn this woman, let it not be said I delivered punishment with undue haste." His narrow gaze swept the crowd. "Do any speak for her? Do any claim her innocent of the crime of elven witchcraft?" the lord bellowed.

Fiadh looked desperately, noting the faces of those her mother must have helped throughout the years. There were women and men who had traded goods for infusions to heal everything from toothache to putrid cuts. Children clutched their mothers' skirts, and Fiadh knew Riona's gentle hands had brought some into this world. But none rose their voices in her defense. No one spoke compassion or innocence. Fiadh's heart stuttered in her breast, growing cold and angry.

Some had the decency to look away, shame and horror marring their faces, while others looked on stoically, not a flicker of humanity in their features. Thoughts of the Cù-Sìth flared in her mind. She could call on them, beg them to intervene. Reaching toward their alien minds, she sent for them, feeling the moment they felt her in their minds.

"If they want a witch," she spat into the air, "I will give them one."

Hate spilled from her eyes as she imagined unleashing the monsters of legend upon the village, sending the Cù-Sìth to save her mother, and let any dare stand in their way. Fiadh's body felt hot, powerful, as she stood waiting for the carnage she would release.

Minutes passed, each agonizing, cooling her anger and fierce heart, as she watched men pile more kindling beneath the platform. They weren't coming, she realized, despair overwhelming her.

She had no choice then. Wrenching herself away from the protection of the forest, Fiadh walked forward, fear coursing through her limbs. *She* would speak for Mother. *She* would remind this cruel assembly of all Riona had done for the people who now stood by cheering for her death. A handful of steps beyond the cover of shadows, she was flung backward, the neck of her gown ripping and exposing her soft flesh. Fiadh yelped and squirmed, flipping onto her stomach and staring at the massive paws of a Cù-Sìth. Her heart thumped in her chest as blood rushed through her ears. For a moment, she could imagine the animal tearing into her, carried away in the heat of the frenzy that filled the village square. Bellows from the men preparing to burn her mother jolted her, and she looked into the yellow stare that blazed above her.

"Please," she begged, her eyes flitting from one animal to another before coming to rest on the one who had pulled her into the forest. "You must help her. They are going to burn my mother. Please."

The Cù-Sìth shifted his attention to the townsfolk, his lip curling. *The hearts of men have not changed.*

Fiadh scrambled to her feet. *Please, Vaymi. Help her.*

I am Krulan. Vaymi is my second. He told her, canting his head to a dark form behind him.

Fiadh nodded. *Will you help her, Krulan?*

We cannot.

What? Why?

We are bound to the wood, just as you are.

"You can't let her die!" she yelled.

It is not for us to intervene.

"Fine, I'll go myself!" Fiadh shouted, but the moment

her feet met the border of the woods, Krulan snatched her back.

You will not put yourself in danger.

"Let me go!" she cried.

But Krulan held her fast, pinning her to the ground beneath his strength and iron will, and she was powerless to stop him.

Fiadh was devastated, struggling against him as sobs tore from her throat.

From the square came a new chant. "Torch her! Burn the elf witch!" Voices rose in bloodlust, the words growing louder with every utterance. Eyes blurry with tears, she watched through the trees as Darragh took the torch himself and lit the nearest bundle.

Fire licked up the wooden block, encircling the platform on which Riona stood before arching upward and catching onto the hem of her woolen dress. As the flames slowly engulfed Riona's form, Fiadh kept her eyes fixed on her mother's head, watching for the slightest hint of awareness and hoping her mother wouldn't awaken to feel her body burn. Fire raced up her clothes, finally reaching the tip of the braid that hung down Riona's shoulder. Moments after the flames started burning her hair, she stirred, her body thrashing in the confines of the ropes holding her fast. Lifting her head away from the heat, she screamed, her cries ending in spastic coughing as smoke filled her lungs. Fiadh lurched forward, straining futilely against Krulan, watching in anguish, her fist stuffed in her mouth, as her mother was swallowed whole in a lake of fire that consumed her utterly.

CHAPTER ELEVEN

Gideon heard her sobbing before she broke through the trees. Stumbling from the hut, he raced toward her as best he could, but his leg gave out, and he fell hard, eyes darting from tree to tree as Fiadh's cries grew louder. Staggering to his feet, he veered in the direction of her voice and called for her.

"Fiadh! Fiadh!" A broken wail came to his ears, and he lurched toward it. "Fiadh!"

As he got closer to the sounds of distress, he swore he saw a mass of dark shapes, but as soon as she came into sight, they were gone. Tears streamed down her face, turning to blubbering sobs as Fiadh found him and swerved toward his open arms.

"They killed her!" she sobbed.

He ran his hands over her shoulders, noting a deep scratch under a rent in her dress. "Who? Fiadh, why is your dress torn? Did someone attack you?"

She shook her head violently. "Mother! They killed her!"

He blanched and wrapped her in a fierce hug as he

scanned the woods. Pulling her toward the hut, he looked back, fearing he'd see a contingent of soldiers bearing down on them. When she was settled inside, the story came out in fits and starts. Ugly. Horrifying.

Fiadh stood in his arms, tugging on his tunic, knuckles turning white as she gripped the fabric. She kept the Cù-Sìth to herself, unable to speak of them, but the rest spilled from her like a poisonous river, and when she finished, she crumpled. He picked her up, laboring under the effort in his weakened state, and sat on a stool, tucking her head against his chest.

Hours later, they sat across from each other in front of the cold hearth. Gideon's body trembled, flooded with fatigue so profound that holding his head up had become too much, and it now hung to his chest. Something had told him he should never have let her leave. Even now, his memories of lurching through the forest in a desperate bid to find her as her cries filled the air were disjointed and pain-filled.

Fiadh had stopped weeping, tears and mucous having dried on her cheeks and the underside of her nose in a salty crust. Looking toward the door which stood open, she thought how her life had been irrevocably changed. "I don't understand how it came to this. What have we ever done but help the people of that village?"

Gideon looked up at her with a pained expression. "Sometimes, there is no understanding. A man, filled with rage and grief, can do unspeakable things to those who fall under his wrathful eye. I'm sorry this has happened. From the little I knew of her, Riona was a good woman, and this was a grave injustice."

"I had never understood the hate people have for others... outsiders... Aos Sí. Mother... she never... she wasn't like that." She shook her head, swallowing hard. "I understand that hatred now."

Gideon frowned. "Some hatred is born of good reason."

"Does it? I suppose, after today, it does for me."

"Fiadh, I know this is not the right time, but you have to understand that once the seeds of suspicion have been sown, they spread like fire. You can't stay here. It's too close to the village."

Fiadh looked away. "When my father and brother died, we came to this forest. Mother told me it was to seek quiet and safety." She shrugged. "I have no memories of life beyond these trees. I can't even recall the faces of papa and Calum." Fiadh's hands clenched, becoming fists. "I now see why she wanted to leave that world. They are evil."

"You would be welcome in Belfirth," Gideon said softly.

She stared at him. "That is not where I belong."

"The people of Felmore have shown you that you don't belong there either."

"Aye, they have shown that." But Felmore wasn't her true home. Dorcha Wood was.

Fiadh reflected on the times she had spent combing through woods, befriending wild things while feeling the heart of the forest beneath her feet, always coming home to the warmth and love of her mother. It pained her to think of leaving. Dorcha Wood had been her haven, content to reveal its secrets to her gentle hands. To consider going felt like a betrayal, and yet the village, those monsters, were so close.

Leaning forward, Gideon took her hands in his. "You aren't safe here, Fiadh. Come to Belfirth."

"This is where Mother and I carved out our life together," she whispered.

"It is also where she was murdered. Just beyond the border of the forest are the people who did this to her. You think they won't do the same to you?"

Rage coursed through her as she thought of being wrenched from her home and thrust into another world full of people who might be no better than the ones who took her mother's life. She welcomed it. It helped with the pain that threatened to crush her. "I wish we had been witches," Fiadh blurted. "I wish we had brought the blight on them! They deserve it! They deserve to pay for what they did to her! All she ever wanted to do was help them. Keep me safe and help them. And they burned her for it!"

Gideon reached for her, wrapping his arms around her as she let the venom out, the righteous anger. She needed to feel it, and he let her. When she grew quiet, he let her go, watching as she curled onto her pallet in an exhausted heap.

CHAPTER TWELVE

*D*arragh called to his guard as he entered the great hall, waiting for them on the dais and glowering at servants who scuttled by. Donal arrived with four men, taking large strides toward his lord and bowing low.

"My lord," he said.

"Donal, it appears you must gather some men to go hunting."

Donal raised his brow. "Aye? Is the larder so low already?"

"It is not for meat that you will hunt… well, perhaps it is," he chuckled, "but not that of a buck. I want you to hunt for the witch's spawn."

"I thought her son died," Donal replied, looking at the man next to him, who nodded slowly.

"Folk say she had a daughter when she lived within my borders, and I want her. Being of the loins of that woman means her evil lives still, and I mean to snuff it out."

"Aye, my lord. I will assemble the men. Where shall they begin their hunt?"

"In Dorcha Wood," Darragh said, sneering as he noticed two of the men going pale. "If that witch has been living there with her child all this time, the men will find her and bring her to me. Unspoiled."

Donal nodded and gave brief instructions to the soldiers who went to do their lord's bidding, then returned to stand at Darragh's feet.

"Donal?" Darragh said.

"Aye, my lord?"

"It occurs to me that my people have known the witch lived and failed to give me word of it. They have sheltered her until her devilry became too much to bear."

Donal nodded slowly.

"I wish for you to find out who was helping her and… bring them to me."

"It will be done, my lord," Donal said and turned on his heel. As he entered the inner bailey, he took a deep breath, ignoring the scent of rotted hay from the stables that permeated the muddy square. He had been Lorcan's captain, having been assigned the post just after earning his spurs. As the fourth son of a noble, there were no lands to inherit, and he had been happy to be appointed under the Lord of Felmore. But his son. Donal shook his head. That one had a hunger for blood and cruelty that would never be quenched.

He sighed and struck off to speak to one of his men and find out who had associated with the witch. It didn't take long to hear of Ohran's farm, those being questioned eager to cast blame on someone else. Finding the elderly man outside, Donal grimaced, knowing the man's age would make no difference to Darragh when it came time for questioning.

"Ohran?" Donal asked, coming up behind the man who flinched, startled by the sudden arrival of soldiers.

"Aye."

"You will come with me," Donal said and jerked his head toward two men who stood a few paces away. They seized Ohran's arms and hauled him to a waiting horse and cart.

"What have I done?" Ohran cried feebly.

"You have aided the witch of Dorcha Wood and will be questioned by your lord."

Ohran's face lost its color, but he said nothing as the men tossed him into the cart. Villagers stopped to watch as he was led through muddy lanes, past Riona's blackened body, a reminder to all of what happened to witches. Ohran glanced at a few of the faces but ducked his head into his arms after one bold youth ran to the cart and spat on him. The ride to the castle was brief. As the horse pulled up to a small door on the castle's lower level, Ohran's fear grew, and his body convulsed. Under Donal's watchful eyes, the soldiers pulled him from the cart and shoved him into the darkness of Felmore Castle's dungeons.

"Please," he begged as Donal stepped around the trio and grabbed a torch, "I have done nothing wrong!"

"Your lord will determine your innocence or guilt. Save your protestations for him."

Donal led the way to a tiny cell, and Ohran was roughly pushed inside. He felt for the stone walls, unable to see more than vague shapes in the dimness, horror growing when his foot crunched on something hard. "I am innocent! Let me out!" he screamed.

The lock of his cell turned with an ominous clang, and

the feeble light from the torch beyond the door receded as the soldiers left him to his fate. Ohran screamed, the sound bouncing off the walls, until he grew hoarse, coughing violently. As emptiness filled the darkness, he listened to womanly laughter drifting through the dank pit and shuddered.

"I can smell you," the voice rasped, "your fear piss and aged blood." Cackling erupted, and he covered his ears. "Do you smell it, Emer?" Giggling followed.

Ohran fumbled toward the cell door and beat on it, fists pounding against the wood until they ached. "Help me! Help me!"

The sound of boots in the corridor stopped his frantic yelling. Ohran listened, pressing his ear to the small opening. "Is someone there?"

A heavy key slipped into the lock, and Ohran stepped back a couple of paces, cringing when his foot brushed against something. Light from a torch filled the room, and a soldier reached into the cell and gripped Ohran by his tunic. Just beyond the doorway stood Lord Darragh.

"Milord," Ohran cried, trying to bend at the waist, "I have done naught, milord. I have not consorted with a witch."

Darragh's scrutiny traveled from the man's head to his feet, pitiless. "Innocent? You claim to be innocent of your crimes?"

"Crimes, milord? What crimes?"

Slipping his sword from its sheath, Darragh spun the weapon in a series of graceful arcs, stopping as the blade touched Ohran's neck. "I have no patience for liars."

Ohran gulped, his legs wobbling. "I speak only truth, milord. I wouldn't tell you a falsehood."

Whipping the blade in a quick upward motion, Darragh sliced open Ohran's chin. The man screeched and tried to pull away, but the soldier who held him kept him immobile. "I see you will require a special interrogation, eh?" Ohran's eyes widened. "Leave us," Darragh said to the soldier.

Ohran sagged against the wall as Darragh walked toward him, a cruel smile curling his lips. "Do I need to prod you with my sword or will you come willingly?"

"I will come, milord."

Darragh nudged him forward, and they made their way to another cell. He watched as the lord of the manor withdrew a large key and unlocked the door, shoving him inside the dimly lit room. The moment he took in the scene, Ohran tried to bolt, but Darragh would have none of it and hooked his legs, sending the man to the floor.

Giggling, the same maniacal laughter he had heard before exploded in the cell, drawing Ohran's horrified gaze to a woman who sat in a darkened corner. Next to her stood another, her bulky form giving the impression of a prisoner's keeper. "She's a witch," Ohran whispered.

Darragh considered his mother for a moment. "Aye, she may very well be, but you shall address her as the Lady of Felmore."

"The lady of… I thought she was dead."

Darragh wrenched Ohran's arm, pulling him roughly to his feet, and herded him toward Haegna. When the man was an arm's length away, Darragh shoved him to the ground and onto his knees.

His mother looked the man up and down, eyes dancing

with lunatic mirth. "I could smell the fear on that one the moment you brought him in," she said. "I don't know what you want of him, but I'll not be drinking his blood and catching the bringer of death that haunts his shadow."

"I want you to look into his mind, Mother. What you do with him after that, I care not."

Scooting to the edge of the chair she sat upon, Haegna reached out her arms, fingers curled like claws.

Ohran balked. "Please, milord. I've been loyal. I would do nothing to harm you or the people of Felmore."

"We shall see," Darragh said, pushing the man's body into Haegna's outstretched hands.

Ohran whimpered with fear at her touch and began babbling, calling to his mother, a woman long dead, to save him from this awful place. His voice ceased as Haegna pressed her nails into his skull, drilling them deeply, blood welling at each small puncture wound. In a low voice, she asked, "What do you know of the witch of Dorcha Wood?"

"She was no witch," he said, thinking of the times Riona had traveled to his farm to trade and chat. "If she were, I had no knowledge of it. She traded with me for what she couldn't forage. That is all."

Haegna looked at her son, giving him a smirk. "Men like to call women with power witches. Isn't that right, son?"

Darragh rolled his eyes. "I want to know of the girl."

She snickered. "The girl. The one you let get away all those years ago? Like her brother?" Haegna tsked. "Shame on you for not plumbing the depths of those woods when the boy was lost to us."

Darragh ground his teeth. "She escaped before I could catch her and her spawn. My spies told me she had left my lands. How was I to know she was but a stone's throw away?"

Ohran's eyes wheeled as he tried to follow their conversation, coming to rest on Haegna as she grinned with a mouth of rotted teeth. "No matter," she said. "If the girl lives, we will find her, and you will bring her to me."

Clenching Ohran's head, she locked eyes with him. He felt flayed open beneath her stare. "Tell me of the girl. The witch's daughter," she said snidely, casting a glance at her son.

"I saw no girl child, nor did Riona speak of one."

Haegna grunted. "He speaks the truth."

Darragh lashed out, knocking a small table onto its side and sending the basin of water atop it hurtling to the floor. "He lies!"

Snickering, Haegna said, "Such a temper, my son, but I assure you he speaks the truth. Of course…"

"What?" Darragh snapped.

"Perhaps, he simply does not know. Women can be secretive," she told him with a sly smile.

Darragh huffed and stalked toward the door. "Do what you will with him. When you're done, send Emer to fetch one of my men to clean up whatever is left." He slammed the door on his mother's chortles of glee mixed with Ohran's pleas for mercy.

CHAPTER THIRTEEN

Fiadh remained quiet after the burning. She often stared into the clearing beyond the hut's threshold as though expecting to see her mother walking up the path. Gideon watched her from a distance, giving her space as he developed a routine to rebuild his muscles and stamina, taking it upon himself to make a crutch and walk in slow passes through sparse sections of the wood or practice with his sword.

But, every shadow of the forest suddenly felt menacing, and he became more and more restless, jumping at the slightest disturbance, unable to take his ease for fear he wouldn't be ready for an attack. Urgency to build up his strength prodded at him, forcing him to wear his sword at all times, as he expected to see a horde of men break through the trees in search of her.

Again and again, Gideon came to Fiadh, who sat listlessly, and tried to explain the dangers, the foolishness of staying, trying to point out that men would surely come, but the girl didn't seem to care or understand. Then, finally, he'd raised his voice, frustration getting the best of him. She'd balked like a frightened fawn, her eyes wide, but she didn't respond in kind, and perhaps that was the worst of it.

No fight. No fire. Nothing.

She just slumped into a ball in the corner of the hovel, her knees tucked against her gently sobbing form. He'd regretted his outburst instantly and rushed to her, uttering apologies and cursing himself as she pulled away from him. At length, his words finally penetrated her grief, and she no longer recoiled when he reached for her.

The evening hours weighed most heavily, and he watched her poke at her food, noting the glances she sent to her mother's empty pallet or the herbs hanging from the rafters. Attempts at conversation led to Gideon doing the bulk of the talking, and he filled the quiet with fanciful stories of the creatures that had once enthralled her. Now, as he spoke of the sluagh or graceful horses with white spiraling horns, she looked vacant, as though she was there, in body, while her mind was somewhere else, though her lips would curve in a slight smile now and then as if she heard and felt something.

Gideon continued the slow path to recovery, and with each new day was the realization that a ravenous mob wasn't coming. Perhaps, she was right, and the people of Felmore feared the woods so much they wouldn't trespass, even for a witch. Gideon refused to become complacent, though, not letting down his guard as he went about the long hours of the day training to regain his strength and the graceful lethality of his skill with a blade.

Mired in shock and grief and not wishing to hear more of why she needed to leave her home, Fiadh withdrew from him, disappearing into the forest. Animals found her, as they always did. Their soft noses pressed her hand or nudged her legs, giving solace as her mind spoke to them, sharing her sadness. Niall, the buck she'd known since girlhood, was a constant companion, shadowing her as she let her feet take her where they would, not caring where she ended up. It was in that daze that she found herself in the last place she would've wished to be.

Fiadh stared at the village square from the cover of the trees, her hands balling into fists. Her mother's burned body, what was left of it, still dangled from the charred pole as though she was not worth the time and effort it would take to pull her down and bury her. Anger bled through her mind, the spark of it causing Niall to bolt into the forest. She ground her teeth, feeding the emotion until it grew into rage.

They will pay for what they did, she thought, glaring at the horrifying remains of her gentle mother.

Bloodlust, a foreign sensation, sang through Fiadh's body, filling it with heat. Her muscles burned, and her heart raced. A black look filled her face. She wanted to charge through the trees like the vengeful witch they claimed she was, laying waste to the people who milled about as though the world hadn't changed when it had. *How dare they! They had no right!*

A low rumble startled her, and she looked to her side, finding three huge bears and a large mountain cat next to them. Glancing at her other side, she saw wolves and foxes, badgers and weasels. Her legs trembled as she realized she had called them. Somehow, she had summoned this army of predators to fight beside her, with no recollection of reaching out to them. An ugly smile lit her face, and a metallic taste filled her mouth. She breathed deeply from her nostrils and turned toward Felmore with a snarl that was echoed by the creatures at her sides.

She took a step forward, feeling each animal take it with her, and raised her arms. At that moment, a small child, a little girl, darted into the scene, her older brother trailing behind her. Fiadh's chest squeezed as she watched the child's braids bounce against her back and heard the tinkle of her laughter carried on the wind. She was innocent, that little girl. All would be slaughtered if she loosed the army at her side onto the village. All. Even the child. With that knowledge came crushing shame. To slay those people would be monstrous. She was not a monster. She was not like *them*.

Reaching out with her mind, Fiadh soothed the beasts standing beside her, calming their wild hearts and sending them back to the safety of Dorcha Wood. She wouldn't become what she had seen in those men. Then, turning away from the remains of her mother, Fiadh retreated, racing through the forest, not caring where she ended up.

CHAPTER FOURTEEN

Four of Darragh's soldiers stood just outside the line of trees marking the border of Dorcha Wood. Fear was stamped on each of their faces as they clenched their swords and sent up prayers to the Great Mother.

One man, no more than a score in age, muttered, "They say monsters live in these woods."

Another scoffed, "What's the matter, Shawn? Are you afraid of fairies and pixies?"

Shawn glowered at his comrade. "All I know is them three went into the woods and didn't come back out."

"Don't you worry, lad, I'll protect your pretty hide."

At the strident bark of an order, the men crossed the threshold and stepped into the dimness of the forest. The trees creaked as their feet thumped on the ground, branches reaching toward them, snagging on their clothes. One man yelped and jumped to the side, knocking into another who shoved him back roughly. Staying close to each other, they moved through the trees, hacking at the limbs that reached for them and tried to force them back. Deeper into Dorcha Wood they traveled until the village disappeared behind them.

A shrill whistle rent the air as one of the men caught sight of something. They gathered, peering into the dimness, and saw a woman, too far away to tell her age, but any woman meandering in this evil place would be of interest to Darragh. Giving a few quick signals, the men took off after her, their long legs eating up the distance in a matter of minutes.

So lost was Fiadh in her thoughts that she wasn't her usual stealthy self and simply wandered with no destination in mind, not thinking of caution, not hearing the soldiers until it was too late. They crashed through the trees, and she looked at them in shock that turned to horror. Spinning away, she lunged forward, her body swept into the air in a cruel grip. The world spun as Fiadh was thrown facedown on the ground.

"Where are you trying to run off to, witch?" one of the men snarled.

Fiadh's eyes darted from one face to another as they formed a loose circle around her. Air whistled from her lungs. There was no mercy in any of them. Rolling to the side, she tried to get to her knees, only to have her arm wrenched as she was flipped onto her back. Fiadh let out a yelp and stared into the face of a man who looked at her with pure malice.

"It was your mother we burned, eh?" the man asked, laughing as she flinched. He must have been her mother's age, hair beginning to grey. He could be someone's father.

"They're gonna burn you too," he whispered, digging his knees into her stomach.

Grabbing her by the hair, he hauled her to her feet and turned toward the other men. "See how easy that was, lads?" They grumbled their agreement, eager to leave the woods.

"Please let me go," Fiadh pleaded, trying to pull her arm from his grasp.

He glared at her and snaked his hand out, slapping her mouth with such force her head flew back. Fear and pain filled her features as she looked, desperate, at the men who stood around her, hoping to find compassion but seeing none.

They dragged her through the forest, yanking her arm when she balked, ignoring every plea. Animals descended, snarling and clawing at men who lashed at them with swords, killing a few who couldn't escape their wicked blades and injuring others who ran away whining. Fiadh screamed as she felt their pain or death, growing more panicked the further they took her. As light bloomed up ahead, filtering through the trees at the edge of the woods, Fiadh grew frenzied, pitting her strength and weight against the man whose brutal grip dug into her soft flesh, and sent out a plea to the Cù-Sìth.

"Fight all you want, witch. When Darragh is done with you, you'll beg for the flames."

His dark promise still hung in the air as Krulan burst through the trees, the pack of Cù-Sìth behind him. The man who held Fiadh had a moment to stare in fear. Just one moment. And then he was ripped from her body as Krulan's massive jaws clamped onto his form, razor-sharp teeth slicing through armor as though it were cloth. Blood splattered across Fiadh's face, feeling sticky. She stumbled and blinked. Her vision blurred, and she realized drops of it hung from her lashes, the liquid hovering just beyond her eyes.

With a shrill scream, Fiadh swatted at her face, trying to get the feel of it off her but only managing to smear it, so it became a gruesome mask. All around her was the sound of flesh tearing, bones cracking, and the stink of death as the Cù-Sìth tore the soldiers to pieces.

It was finished in seconds, leaving the woods ominously silent. Fiadh glanced at Krulan and the others, but her attention strayed to the mangled remains littering the ground. She doubled over and vomited. Krulan moved toward her bent form, watching as her neck contorted in violent spasms until she grew still and hung her head limply.

Are you hurt? he asked.

She shook her head. *How could you do that? Kill them… like that?* her mind pleaded.

If we had not come, they would have taken you.

But you didn't have to kill them. They would have run at the sight of you.

There is only death when men meet Cù-Sìth. Ours, or theirs.

Why?

Men may not see us and live to tell of it.

Fiadh's mouth worked, but no sound came out. It was too much. This was too much. She looked down at her hands, saw the dark red stains, and rubbed them on her skirts. She *was* a monster, after all.

She left the clearing on unsteady legs, the Cù-Sìth at her sides like sentinels, stopping at a small creek on the way to her home. Fiadh washed away the worst of the gore under watchful eyes. *What will Gideon say when he sees me?* she wondered as she scrubbed, cringing at the clots that clung to her skin.

It matters not what he says, Krulan responded, though Fiadh hadn't realized she had sent the thought to him.

"It matters to me," she whispered.

You are under my protection.

"I didn't want this," she said limply. Rising to her feet, Fiadh looked at Krulan, noting the red tinge around his muzzle. "You cannot kill for the sake of killing. If that is what you mean by protection, I want no part of it. I'm not... I don't want to become the demon they think I am."

You are what you are. What you wish to be matters not.

Stop telling me what doesn't matter! She fumed, thinking how Gideon, and now Krulan, were prodding her with what she had to do, who she had to be, never considering what she wanted.

With that, she left them, listening to their churning thoughts as she slowly walked home. *Gideon couldn't know of this. She must think of something to explain the blood,* Fiadh told herself, a plan forming as the hut came into view.

Gideon was sitting on a stool by the fire, using a stone to sharpen the edge of his sword when he looked up. "You've been go—" he dropped the sword and sprang toward her, running his hands along her arms. "What happened? Are you alright?"

Fiadh gently pushed his hands away and stepped around him. "I am fine. The blood isn't my own. Some of Lord Darragh's soldiers decided it would be good sport to hunt a doe and her fawn. This is their blood," she told him, sweeping her hand along her dress. "I must put on something clean. Would you step outside?"

He frowned, looking her up and down, zeroing in on her face. "What of this?" he asked and turned her chin toward the light from the open door.

She licked her bottom lip, feeling the swelling. "The fawn died, and the doe was mad with grief. She fought me and must have struck my mouth."

Gideon looked unconvinced but didn't press her and stepped outside. He listened as Fiadh sifted through her belongings and wondered if there was any truth to her story. He suspected she, and not a deer, may have had a run-in with soldiers. Though, if that were true, how she had gotten away was a mystery. He needed to get her far from here, to the safety of Belfirth. She wouldn't want to hear it again, but they must go. And soon.

CHAPTER FIFTEEN

The next day, having escaped Gideon's watchful eye, Fiadh sat atop a boulder overlooking a large swath of the forest. A hawk flew low in the sky, its body dark against the backdrop of the late morning sun. It circled lazily, in broad swoops, not searching for prey so much as feeling the wind beneath its wings and reveling in it. She closed her eyes and felt it too. Freedom. As Fiadh followed its progress, she sensed a stirring in the air around her, a familiar disturbance like a balm as it coalesced into a presence unseen and unheard.

"Danu," she whispered, her breath spilling out in a thin fog, "I feel lost."

Fingers of air stroked her face in tender caresses, so like her mother's sweet touch that tears pooled and spilled down her cheeks. A sob lodged in her throat as she clenched her teeth against it, leaning her face into breaths of wind that finally broke her will, releasing the grief in hoarse cries. There were no words. Never had there been in all the time

Fiadh had reached out to the Great Mother. But words were unnecessary things, abrasive and easily twisted. This was deeper. Honest. Pure.

She let it out, all the anguish and anger, in torrents of sobbing and curses that wracked her body and left her head an aching mass, all the while feeling she wasn't alone. A different mother was there. The mother of all things and this mother felt, loved, grieved alongside Fiadh. But she didn't feed the rage in Fiadh's heart. Danu was the embodiment of life, not the bringer of death Fiadh craved for those who had taken Riona's life. There was no scolding of Fiadh's dark wishes, only understanding for the sorrow that produced them. It was that gentle presence that broke through the anger and left Fiadh hollowed out.

When tears finally turned to ugly hiccups, Fiadh wiped her face upon her loose sleeve, whispering gratitude to Danu in stilted words whose meaning went deeper than the syllables that formed them. The Great Mother left then, her presence retreating onto the wind, rustling through the leaves with noises which almost sounded like speech. Almost.

Niall, his antlers casting shadows upon the ground, drifted toward Fiadh from the safety of the trees, adding his solace in gentle nuzzles and soft huffs. She ran her hands along his velvety fur, feeling the corded muscles ripple under her touch.

"Thank you, my friend," she whispered.

The buck bumped her shoulder, a low sound rumbling in his chest. *This is who I am*, Fiadh thought. *This is where I belong, not tucked away in walls of stone in a land so distant from here that I had never heard of it until Gideon spoke its name.* But as soon as the idea took root, aching loneliness consumed her, dampening the determination that had suffused her body only moments before. To imagine living in her small hut alone filled her with dread. More soldiers would come. Or vengeful men seeking to cast blame for the next blight or famine.

Stay.

Leave.

The pull from both tugged at her mind and heart with neither giving ground. Fiadh's head ached, and she sighed, leaning against Niall's body, matching her breath to the slow pull of his. This was real, the blood pumping through the limbs of an animal whose mind could speak to hers without the need for words and subterfuge. It was truth. Untainted.

Could she ever have that with Gideon? Their connection was tenuous, but even she could feel it growing, and there *could* be a future with him if she had the courage to reach for it. But for that to become even a shadow of reality, he should understand all she was, those intimate parts of herself, perhaps even more than what she had shared with Mother. The knowledge that she might open herself to him so entirely caused anxiety to flood her body, and within that were the sounds of screams and the scent of charred flesh. What if she told him about her connection to Dorcha Wood and the wild things that called it home? Of the Cù-Sìth? What if, upon learning this, he turned his back on her, as the people of Felmore had turned their backs on her mother?

What if she kept those parts hidden and joined him to escape the solitude standing before her like a lone sentry?

There was some appeal in the notion, but that draw was quickly swallowed by the knowledge that concealing who she was until she lost the pieces which defined her, becoming an empty shell to fit the vision of a man who knew her not, was a path she couldn't travel. Maybe the wood was to be her life, and she alone in it. Fiadh sighed and rose, her mind no closer to a decision. The anger and grief no closer to healing.

The sun sank, and mother moon rose, taking the warmth and light of the day. Gideon stood just within the threshold of the hut, listening as Fiadh puttered about since her return from wherever she had gone for long hours of the day. His legs had begun to cramp from the exercise he had forced on himself to regain his strength. It was clear he had overdone it and his muscles spasmed in painful waves. Standing was the only means of relief. As he watched evening's shadows descend, a huge wolf entered the small clearing. It was smokey grey with yellow eyes that bore into him as he stood frozen. Poking her head around his frame, as though she could somehow sense the presence of the silent predator, Fiadh gave a small cry of welcome, launching herself around his body. The sound and movement unlocked Gideon's rigid muscles, and he roughly drew Fiadh back before she could set foot out the door, brandishing his sword, which she batted away before shoving him aside and walking toward the beast. Kneeling at the wolf's head, she spoke softly as they looked into each other. Gideon's hand tightened on the hilt of his sword, and his heart raced as the animal sniffed her hair while she stroked his fur. It was unnerving.

"Fiadh, come away from him," he whispered.

"I shall do no such thing. Faolan would never hurt me." She wrapped her arms around the animal, shushing the wolf as he sent a low growl at Gideon.

He watched, clenching his teeth as he imagined the beast's massive jaw ripping through the flesh she so carelessly exposed. With a final caress through his thick pelt, she stood, staring after the wolf as it trotted into the forest. Fiadh viewed her actions as normal, as evidenced by her admonition of his attempts to stop her, but he had never witnessed such a communion. Gideon wondered if there was more to her than what he saw. *Aos Sí.* He felt guilt the moment the thought formed, but it was there.

Kernels of doubt took root.

Could Riona have learned the ways of the Aos Sí? Had she been an elven witch? It seemed preposterous, as that race was nearly obliterated during the Great War, but what if, somehow, their blood and ways were passed along to some small few in this mystical forest? It was no secret Dorcha Wood was the last stronghold of a genuinely devious elf king, a being whose cunning and treachery had resulted in the ambush and slaughter of thousands of men.

And if Riona had been using the ways of the Aos Sí, could her daughter have remained ignorant of her dabbling in those forbidden arts?

"Did you find the wolf as a pup?" he blurted.

Her brow wrinkled. "What do you mean?"

"I've heard of men finding wolf pups and raising them as pets."

She laughed. "Faolan isn't my pet."

"So, you didn't raise him?" Gideon asked.

Fiadh shook her head.

"Then how are you able to get so close?"

Shrugging, Fiadh stepped inside to prepare a meal, leaving Gideon to wonder what he witnessed and what it could mean. After stewing for a few useless minutes, Gideon shut his mind to his dark thoughts. He closed the door on the night and his misgivings and settled into the quiet routine which had taken shape as he recuperated.

As he watched her bustle about in the cramped space, he marveled that he was even welcomed here, alone with an unmarried woman, though that is not how it began. Fiadh appeared to have no qualms about sharing her home with him—essentially a male stranger. He wondered if she ever worried he would take advantage. She seemed utterly oblivious of societal rules governing everyone outside this tiny corner of the world, rules that would view this living situation as improper, forcing Fiadh to become an outcast should word spread. She would be labeled a whore and shunned by those who saw themselves in the moral right if they were found out.

He tried to broach this subject with her as she spooned food into a bowl, but she waved away his worry. "I care nothing for what people would say of me."

"You don't worry what some may think of us living unchaperoned, should they find out?"

"Why should I care? It mattered not that my mother had done nothing. They saw evil when there was none!"

He watched her slam the spoon down too hard, globs of soft vegetables splattering on the small table.

"I have seen enough of the world beyond my woods to know evil lurks *there*, not here!" she spat.

"I'm sorry, Fiadh. I didn't mean to upset you," he said soothingly. "You are innocent and kind, and I would have only good things to say of the woman I have come to know."

She huffed and sat with a thump. "It's not you that I'm angry with."

"I know."

"If others want nothing more than to see evil where there is none, what can I do to change that?" she asked.

Gideon thought for a moment. Hatred for the Aos Sí ran deep, and some looked for it. Sadly, some found it when it was never there, to begin with. As the idea surfaced, he realized that he had been one of those people, seeing her strange connection with the animals of Dorcha Wood and linking it to those cursed peoples. At times, he was no better than the angry mob that murdered Riona, seeing evil where it didn't exist.

"I don't know how to change the minds of so many," he finally said. "How do you stop a flood?"

Fiadh muttered under her breath and picked up her bowl. They ate in silence for a while, and eventually, her shoulders relaxed, and the heat of anger left her face.

I should stop worrying about what I cannot change, Gideon told himself. *And stop seeing things that aren't there,* he silently added.

Putting thought into action, he focused on the small things Fiadh did and said as the evening wore on, the quiet conversation after supper when the fire crackled in the hearth. As he coaxed her into a light-hearted conversation, he noted the bruise along her mouth had become a light purple, barely visible now, and eyed it suspiciously. Let her have her secrets, he decided, biting his tongue. Soon, he would take her from this place, and she would never again fall victim to ruthless men.

CHAPTER SIXTEEN

Time passed quickly as Gideon pushed himself in his recovery, forcing his body up and out to take short walks, now more often with Fiadh at his side. When he trained, she sat and watched. Every swing of his sword grew stronger as the grueling hours wore on, and soon it spun through the air with deadly skill. With the strengthening of his muscles came relief that should a contingent of Darragh's men find them, he could hold them off long enough for Fiadh to get to safety.

In quiet moments, Fiadh and Gideon spoke of different things, telling stories of their youth, getting to know each other on an intimate level. Gideon would often regale her with humorous escapades he and Doran had put their parents through to chase away the sadness haunting her. From stealing a piglet to keep as a pet—a venture that ended with two mud-covered boys running through the great hall as the squealing animal overturned a small table and sent more than one servant sprawling to the floor—to sneaking into the larder to eat an entire jar of honey before being discovered by the cook who had followed a line of ants as they sat in a puddle of the sweet treat. The stickiness of that event took days to remove from the larder's cracks and crevices, and cook had banned both boys from entering the kitchen for a full two years. Gideon relished the smiles and quiet laughter the accounts brought as hours stretched into days.

During this time, the depth of her unusual kinship with wild things became even more apparent. Animals had begun to show themselves within his presence with regularity. However, he did not attempt to reach for them as she did, having retained his wariness in light of a wild animal's unpredictability. It was wondrous and strange to watch, but he feared for her, knowing the capriciousness of beasts.

"Have they always come to you?" Gideon asked as they moved to a cluster of berry bushes that held the last of the fall harvest.

Fiadh paused, looking up from the porcupine that had lumbered to her side for a handful of the tart crop. She stroked his nose, the only truly safe place to pet such an unusual creature, and stood to face him. "One of my first memories is that of a doe and fawn. I don't recall the events myself, only images really, but Mother would tell me the story so often as a child I feel those recollections are my own."

Gideon smiled, settling against the trunk of a tree so he could watch her as the giant oak took the brunt of his weight, giving his weary legs much-needed rest. "I was very young," she began, "having passed my third year when I was in the clearing outside our home and the two animals found me. Mother said it was as though they were drawn to me."

Fiadh looked at Gideon, heartened to see he was genuinely interested in an ability she had been reluctant to share. "The doe left the shelter of the trees and shrubs, an act that in itself is contrary to their nature, and brought her fawn to my outstretched hand. Mother had never seen the like, or so she would tell me, and swore that was when my affinity manifested because, after that day, I was rarely without the company of wild things."

"And Riona, did she have the same kinship?"

"She never spoke of it, and I never witnessed such." She shrugged. "Mayhap it's just me. My mother…" Fiadh paused, her features aching with sorrow as she swallowed a lump of grief, "encouraged it at first, but as the years passed and my connection grew stronger, I would often see worry in her face. At times, she tried to curb my behavior, but when pressed for reasons, she would grow quiet, and, more often than naught, those talks ended with me running into the woods anyway. I admit," Fiadh chuckled softly, "to being quite willful."

The porcupine sniffed the ground at Fiadh's feet before toddling away, stopping only once to look at Gideon and offering a series of high-pitched squeals, grunts, and chirps that sounded less than friendly. Gideon stood silent under the animal's odd rebuke and waited for it to disappear into the forest. A thought popped into his head once the large rodent was swallowed in the undergrowth, and he turned to Fiadh. "Do you know what the animal said?"

A shadow fell across Fiadh's face as though an invisible curtain had dropped, clouding her eyes. "Not in words. It is more an impression of feeling than anything else," she told him, but he couldn't help wondering if that was the whole truth, and his suspicion bothered him.

Unsettled by his question, Fiadh resumed picking berries in silence, and soon they returned to the warmth of the hearth, eating a small meal as darkness settled into the woods, making small talk until the length of the day brought on the inevitable weariness, calling them to their pallets. Fiadh curled up against the wattle and daub wall, the place Riona had slept, tucking her woolen blanket over her head to keep out the chill. She listened to the sounds of Gideon turning this way and that, finding the perfect groove in the padding which would allow his body to rest. Eventually, he stilled, his breath puffing softly in the night.

Fiadh reviewed all she had shared with him that day and wondered what he honestly thought of her gift. She couldn't help but see his suspicion, not that he could hide it anymore. They had come to know each other as she hadn't known anyone, aside from Mother. And what would her mother say if she knew what Fiadh had divulged? She huffed, imagining the scolding she would have received, the warnings of wagging tongues and suspicion, of blind hatred and vilification. Until Riona had become the target of it, Fiadh had never taken them seriously. To her, it had always seemed exaggerated, the imaginings of an overprotective parent. Though she had followed her mother's rules to the point of utter loneliness, she had always assumed most people were good and just in her heart. But, now? Now, the façade was lifted, and the ugliness she had been warned of had come to fruition.

Rolling over, she looked at Gideon, hearing the soft rumble of his snores. In sleep, he looked boyish, the lines of worry and fatigue fading into smooth innocence beneath his thickening beard. But if he were to open his eyes, she would see doubt tickling at the edges, which frightened her. Yet, more than the doubt were the other things she saw, deeper feelings, and Fiadh wondered if he saw them within her too.

CHAPTER SEVENTEEN

On a bright morning, Gideon knew it was time to leave. He felt it, and he had always listened to his instincts. Too many days had passed, and the blight persisted. The villagers would become restless, and they could perceive any unusual illness or death as the work of Riona's daughter. Her safety was in jeopardy, though she refused to see it. Gideon decided he would take her with him, his heart lost among her smiles and compassion. Now, all that remained was convincing her to leave this place before it was too late.

"Fiadh." She turned to look at him, her apron filled with eggs from the small coop. "We must go."

"Oh, not this again," she sighed. "And where do you wish me to go?"

Setting the eggs in a basket, she joined him on the large tree trunk that lay on its side. A layer of moss blanketed the bark, adding a cushion of softness to the rough surface. Thinking of the times she had sat on this very spot with her mother was bittersweet.

"To Belfirth. I want you to come with me."

She looked around, agonizing over the choice facing her. She wasn't ready. This moment had come too soon. "I've told you I can't leave. This is my home."

"You're not safe here, Fiadh." Gideon took her hand, momentarily marveling at how small her fingers were within his grasp. She was too innocent of the ways of the world, too sheltered in this infamous wood her mother had raised her in. "They'll come for you, too."

Staring into him, she watched a play of emotions in his face. There was genuine worry, but she saw a possessiveness that was new to her within that. It made her uneasy.

"The people of Felmore know nothing of my existence."

But she knew that was not true. Soldiers had come. And they would come again, and when that happened, she would call on the Cù-Sìth. But… if she summoned them, it would lead to blood. Death. Already, four men had been killed because of her. If she stayed, more would die. *Is that what I want?* she thought. *Could I live with that?*

"I know you believe they do not know of you," Gideon said, "but you told me your family once lived within the village. Do you honestly feel it has been forgotten?"

Fiadh made a face. "I haven't been seen in years," she lied. "They will think I am dead if they remember me at all."

Gideon shook his head. "The elders will know of you. Their memories are long."

She huffed. "Why do you want me to go with you?"

"I want to keep you safe, and I can't do that here. With the strength of my family, you will be protected and want for nothing."

"Are you so certain they would welcome me? An outsider?"

He muttered blackly, "I will ensure they do."

Laughing at his mumbling, she stood, walking the span of the clearing. Every piece of this place was part of her, her history, who she was. Even without her mother, she still belonged to this forest, just as it belonged to her. Fiadh knew Gideon wouldn't understand. He felt no connection to the woods, but there was something. She felt strong within their boundaries, as though Dorcha Wood was connected to her very being like it somehow fused its life force with hers. To leave meant severing that relationship.

Her mind drifted as she looked to the north, thinking of the Cù-Sìth who lived in anonymity in a territory Krulan had referred to as Erabel. Why she thought of them, she couldn't say, but it suddenly felt important. Was she meant to remain here and forge a bond with them? What had Krulan said that day when his pack had taken the bodies of Darragh's men? He knew who she was. Wasn't that strange? Why would he know of her? She was no one of importance. And again, when they had slain Darragh's men, he had said he would protect her, as though it was a role he had been given.

Gideon clearing his throat brought her back to the present.

She returned to his side. "You aren't well enough to travel, and you have no horse." He cocked his head but didn't argue as she continued, "Isn't it a fair distance to your home?"

Catching her meaning, he took her hand. "You cannot

sway me. We will find horses along the way. I'll steal them if I must, though I do have coin."

"They hang horse thieves."

"Only if they catch them," Gideon countered with a wink. "I won't leave you here, Fiadh."

"Has your memory returned?"

The question took him by surprise. "Nay, though it feels like I dream my memories. I just can't keep hold of them when I wake." Stroking her fingers, he added, "But you will not distract me. We must go."

She sighed, turning away. "You make it sound as though this is just a place like any other, but it isn't." Pulling her hand from his, she clenched her fists in her dress, twisting the woolen fabric in her fingers. "Part of me wants to go with you, start a new life." Fiadh looked at him. "But the larger part of me cannot endure the thought of leaving. It's hard to explain, and I don't know that you would understand." She swept her arms outward, encompassing the immediate land-scape. "The woods are more than what you see, there is a heart in it, and my life beats in time with its pulse."

Gideon let out a long sigh of frustration. "Fiadh, I can't leave you. You don't understand the evils of men and I—"

She rounded on him, eyes sparking. "I don't understand the evils of men? I saw men burn my mother!"

Holding up his hands, Gideon said, "I apologize. You have beheld that ugliness."

Fiadh looked somewhat mollified.

He spoke slowly, trying to be careful with his words. "What I mean is you don't understand that men… they will never leave you in peace. They will come for you again and again, no matter how well you hide and evade them. They'll keep coming, keep hunting until eventually, they find you. And you will be powerless to stop them."

"You've implied I am unable to care for myself," she snapped, "I may be sheltered from the things you have experienced in your travels or in war, but don't mistake that for weakness."

"You aren't weak, and I am sorry if I have insinuated as much. I did not mean it that way, but you have never left this place, known the world beyond the borders of Felmore."

Fiadh couldn't argue with his reasoning. He was right. She had never ventured into the realms of men that grew outside her small corner of the world. The idea of seeing those places had never appealed to her. Now, even more. Felmore had shown enough of those evils, and she had no desire to see more of it. If that meant she was too sheltered for his world, then she ought to stay here where she was familiar with every rock and tree, where she knew the ways of the forest and the wild things that dwelled there. Where there were some things which frightened even hardened men.

"You're right. I have never seen what lies beyond the village."

"Then you will come with me," he said with relief.

"Nay."

Standing abruptly, Gideon stalked across the clearing, mumbling to himself before striding back to her with huge steps. "Do you know what men will do to you if they find you here alone? Have you any notion of what *I* could do if I had a mind to?"

Flinching from his anger, Fiadh scooted away from him, taking up a spot on the edge of the log. "I am not a fool."

"Staying here is the epitome of foolishness!" Anger flared across her face, and Gideon held up his hands, seeing her mouth curl with a retort. "I'm sorry. I don't mean to anger you. Please, do not mistake my comment for anything, but care for your person." Fiadh's eyes flashed, but she held silent. Sighing, he sat beside her, collecting himself for a few moments. "In my father's time, a woman, much like your mother, was accused of elven witchery when a neighbor's flock died suddenly of an unknown malady. The townsfolk, already suspicious of the sharp-tongued woman, beat her husband and dragged her from her home in the dead of night before hanging her from a tree just outside the borders of Belfirth. My father interceded when word came to him and convened a tribunal for those involved. But the damage had already been done. Days after the woman was hanged, her three daughters were found drowned, bound and gagged, their bodies having been tethered to rocks and thrown into a brook. Their crime? Being the daughters of a woman, the villagers had deemed an Aos Sí witch."

The anger Fiadh had been holding left her in a gush. "That is an awful story."

She looked away, considering what his horrifying tale really meant for her future. It seemed as though this irrational hatred and fear were so pervasive that it mattered little where she lived. And if that were true, why leave?

"Aye, but it should serve as a warning. That incident occurred long ago, but its root, the emotions that stirred in the hearts of angry men, thrives today. You saw it. You saw what the masses did to your mother, a woman whose gentle hands had nurtured the sick and brought babes into the world. How can you truly believe they won't come for you?"

Tears pooled as Gideon's words hit their mark, spreading through her mind. She had no desire to end up tied to a stake, her flesh set alight as people cheered. "I can't trust they won't. I know that." Her shoulders drooped. "It feels as though you are forcing me to make a choice which goes against everything in me." Fiadh looked at him, seeing resolve beneath his veneer of hard living.

"Please leave this place. Come with me before it's too late," he pleaded.

Images of the butchery of the soldiers who had accosted her filled her mind. The Cù-Sìth would come to her aid should anyone seek to do her harm. She knew that. Krulan had made it clear. In this, she was safe, though the cost and weight of guilt at the death of so many was high. But what of her daily life? Already, the grain and other provisions the forest didn't provide had begun to run low, and anxiety had taken their place in her gut. Mother was no longer here to trade for the things they couldn't grow or forage. What food she had brought home from the last visit would have sustained them for longer, but Gideon consumed twice what Mother had. And now? With winter coming and trading in the village impossible, what would become of her? Hatred for the people that led her to this point burned in her chest. *They* should be the ones worried about the crows of starvation, not her.

"They have taken my freedom," Fiadh said.

"Who?"

"Every silent witness. Every accuser. All of them! I... I hate them," she said the last as a sob tore up her throat.

Gideon wrapped his arms around her. "You have every right to hate them."

Reaching out a hand, Gideon tucked strands of dark hair behind Fiadh's ear as she spent her grief, tracing her earlobe with the tip of his finger and traveling up to the malformed tip, her one physical flaw on an otherwise perfect form. Both of her ears had such scars, and he had wondered at it, thinking perhaps she had come to harm as a child and her mother had taken a needle to her flesh before she had honed her skill. Reaching around her head to stroke the other, he felt along the ridges and grooves, noting how they folded over a bit at the weight of their thickness. Fiadh pulled away, tugging long, black strands over her ears.

"Show me," he whispered, brushing her hair back.

She relented, bending her neck so he could see them fully. "They are ugly."

He shook his head. "They are part of you, and not a part of you is ugly."

Why was her heart suddenly beating so fast? Her breathing so shallow? She could feel him staring, still staring, could feel his breath as he leaned in closer, closer, and then ever so gently, she felt his lips brush against her scars, a touch far lighter than she'd have thought him capable of. "Every part of you is beautiful," he whispered.

Pulling away, she rubbed her face with her sleeve and looked around, reluctant to meet his gaze.

"You do no need to fear me, Fiadh. I would never do you harm."

"I know." Turning toward him, she asked, "If I were to come with you, would you let me go if your people turned me away?"

Gideon nodded, though inside, he knew he would never let it come to that.

"Then," she paused, "I will join you."

Relief filled his face. "Thank you, Fiadh. I know how hard it must be to say goodbye to your home." All she could do was nod mutely. "We will leave at midday."

Rising on legs that wobbled, she looked at this small pocket of the world. Turning her face to the side, she told Gideon, "I would like to walk through Dorcha Wood one last time before we go."

Without waiting for a reply, she left the clearing and let her feet take her where they willed. The trees overhead cast strange shadows on the forest floor, matching her mood with their grayness. Her strides slowed as the ground began its subtle slant, taking her to a spot she knew well. The overlook rested on a cliff above a winding stream, giving her a sheltered view of Dorcha Wood. The forest would never reveal all of its secrets, no matter the height or angles at which you viewed her. But from this vantage, she could see stretches of trees and rocks that had provided safety and adventure throughout her life. Perching herself upon the smooth surface of the large boulder jutting above the precipice, she said her goodbyes, even to the Cù-Sìth, spilling her heartache into the wind which took her words and carried them away.

CHAPTER EIGHTEEN

From the shadows, Xander's hungry eyes watched Fiadh, taking her measure, weighing the risk of slitting her throat and angering his master, with the homicidal urge to wet his blade with her blood, sweetly gutting her like a sacrificial lamb and infusing the power of her essence into his spellcraft for years to come. The mage saw her lips move, unable to hear the words she uttered as they were carried on the breeze that sifted through her hair, wafting her innocence to his waiting nostrils where he breathed it in, aching with violence.

It would not please his master should he come from the shadows and slip his knife into her pale neck, but the desire was building, calling to him like the sirens of legend. Tugging his dark cloak over his head, he reached forward, parting branches without a sound, intent on the unguarded form that sat hunched as though she tried to keep herself from falling apart.

The mage whet his lips and rose slowly, unfurling like a menacing shadow with the ravenous gaze of a predator whose unwary prey is captured in its sight. A ritual blade, adorned with runes of power, appeared in his hand from the depths of his black cloak, winking in the weak light breaking through the needles of the pine. His master would forgive him, and if not, the power in her blood would be enough to sustain him should he need to flee, exile himself in the far reaches of the world. Perhaps, if her blood were as potent as he sensed, he could become the master.

Xander broke from the covering of the thicket in which he had hidden, stepping silently onto the needle-littered ground that muted his movements. His baleful stare fixed on Fiadh, bottomless dark eyes peering at her from beneath the hood. Gripping the hilt in his hand, Xander slunk forward and left the protection of the overhanging branches, body suddenly going rigid as a sound, low and menacing, drifted through the forest floor and into his body, causing the hair on the back of his neck to stand on end.

It cannot be! His mind screamed.

Unlocking his rigid form, he turned his head and hissed, spying the hulking beast that stalked him, its lips curled above dagger-like teeth, yellow eyes boring into his hooded form with ancient knowledge. Spinning in a blur of movement, Xander muttered an incantation and launched himself into the forest, casting spells of concealment as the Cù-Sìth pursued him. He raced through the trees, veering to the border in the north where the beast wouldn't dare to cross. Low growls followed the pounding of his feet, and he hurled spells at the creature, a cruel smile curling his lips when he heard it yelp.

The thundering of the beast's paws slowed and finally ceased. Xander ceased his frantic retreat and spat foul oaths into the air as his face filled with hatred. Grinding his teeth, he let the rage spill from his hands and lips, scorching the earth around where he stood until his anger was spent. He would inform his master of the girl and her protector, and perhaps he would linger just beyond these woods and await the man who would soon hunt him.

CHAPTER NINETEEN

Fiadh returned, face flushed, and hurried inside. What had the Cù-Sìth chased, as they tore from the trees a few paces from where she had been sitting? Had there been a soldier? Unease filled her. She should have been more careful. If the Cù-Sìth hadn't been there... if soldiers had taken her... Fiadh shuddered and began packing her things.

"Are you well?" Gideon asked.

"Aye, just… just feeling nervous about leaving."

Gideon said nothing as he watched her for a few moments and then stepped outside with a newly sharpened knife and his leather armor tucked under his arm.

Packing for the journey was finished too soon, and the inevitable outcome of relenting to Gideon's logic and pressure stared Fiadh squarely in the face. She was leaving. Clenching her teeth, Fiadh stepped outside, shutting the door softly behind her. She stepped to the tiny chicken coop and coaxed the hens to her hand, petting them as they squatted while saying goodbye. They would have to forage on their own now, and she knew it was unlikely they would last the night. Standing, Fiadh looked around, drinking everything in and pocketing it away to take out and think of later.

A rustling snagged her attention, and she watched as Gideon came from the direction of the stream and entered the clearing on legs which had regained much of their strength, though she noted the limp in his gait. Fiadh stared at him, dumbfounded. Gone was the scraggly beard that had concealed his face, leaving him youthful and strikingly handsome with a firm jaw and full lips that curved at the corners in a hint of a smile. The scar trailing his left cheek stood out starkly, dark pink and raised against his weathered skin, but did not detract from his appeal. It made him look dangerous, causing her heart to increase in tempo as he stood looming over her. A warrior stood before her now, chiseled and powerful.

"You shaved," she blurted.

"Aye. It was time to rid myself of that growth." His hand reached up to touch the scar, and he turned away, clearly discomfited by her stare.

"Don't," she said, reaching toward him as a blush stained her cheeks, "yours is a very handsome face."

His eyes widened briefly, then crinkled. "Aye?"

Fiadh nodded, fitting a thick cloak around her shoulders before reaching down to grab her supplies. "Shall we go?"

They each slung a large basket with thick leather straps onto their backs, leaving their hands free. Grabbing a walking stick, Gideon stepped aside and beckoned her forward. "Lead the way, milady."

She inhaled deeply, filling her lungs with the rich smells

of the forest. Fiadh imagined the spirit of every wild thing as tiny points of light dotting the complicated fabric of the woodland, and to each point, she bade farewell. To Riona, she flooded her mind with thoughts of love, images of their life together, soft touches, and quiet conversations. It hurt to think words of parting and know their truth, but she did it, and when she'd finished, she took her first step, leading Gideon toward the meadow where she had found him days that felt like years earlier.

The pace Fiadh set was intentionally slow due to Gideon's healing wounds. He grumbled at it at first but soon grew silent as their steps ate up the forest floor. She listened to his breathing, mindful of the strain he was putting on himself. When he tripped over a gnarled root, she stopped, pretending to fix the straps anchored to her shoulders while he shook off the ache in his leg. They carried on and soon came to the edge of Dorcha Wood. Fiadh stopped. The forest pulled at her, tugging insistently, trying to draw her back within its folds. With trembling legs, she stepped over that invisible line and felt a wrenching sadness, not entirely her own, fill her. Craning her neck, she looked back and said goodbye.

A meadow was laid out before them, the place where grasses had been soaked with blood, before becoming patches of displaced earth. Nothing remained of the skirmish but soil dotted with newly grown grasses where the bodies had fallen.

Gideon looked around, taking in the scene and recalling the events that took place there. "I remember being set upon by three men," he said, crouching down painfully to press his hand on the place where Jarvis had been slain. "But I cannot recall how I came to be here. It's muddled."

Fiadh set her basket down, relishing the freedom of movement she felt without its weight. Joining him, she looked at the ground, thinking of the Cù-Sìth she had called to this place. She hadn't told Gideon and had no plans to divulge anything now. Like others, he would not understand.

Placing a hand on Gideon's shoulder, she pulled him out of his reverie. "Do you know the way to your holding?"

He stood slowly. "It lies in the east."

Fiadh nodded and readied herself. Squinting against the sun, she spotted a lone rider bearing down on them. Tugging Gideon, she pointed. "Someone comes."

Gideon turned, swore, and pulled his blade from its sheath. "Get back, Fiadh!"

Watching the horse and rider barrel toward them, her legs felt watery. Darragh wouldn't stop. More men would come. Her haven, the forest that had sheltered her for years, had become tainted by their lust for blood, and she realized as she watched the man come closer that nothing, not even the Cù-Sìth, would stop him. For whatever reason, Darragh wanted her. Eyes darting to the woods, she considered fleeing into their darkness, letting the trees offer whatever protection they could. It would buy them time. But the sound of hooves grew louder, pulling her attention back to Gideon, who stood, with legs braced apart, sword at the ready.

"We should hide," she pleaded. "I know the forest. There are hundreds of places we could—"

"I will not run from this," Gideon said grimly, gripping the haft.

The soldier leaned forward, stretching his body along the neck of his mount, a sneer curling his lip. Fiadh felt the ground shake and watched in horror as the steed rode straight for Gideon. She shrieked as the horse bore down on him, wanting to avert her gaze so she wouldn't have to see his body trampled into the dirt. Gideon shifted and swung his arm at the last moment, the sword slicing through the animal's neck. The horse screamed, its mind blaring red with terror and pain. The force of it slammed into Fiadh, and she fell to her knees as the animal's inhuman screeching filled the air, consuming everything. She covered her ears, trying to block the sound, but it was in her, carving itself into her brain.

The soldier rolled a short distance from the flailing hooves and shrieks of his mount. Gideon gave no quarter advancing within moments, his blade slamming into the guard's with such force the impact split the air, momentarily cutting through the bawling of the dying animal.

Fiadh's head swam with agony, tethered to the horse in a way she had never experienced, and as the animal's life bled out into the soil, she felt her heart squeeze and slow until their connection abruptly severed. She gasped, pulling her attention from the horse and back to the ring of blades a few paces away. Despite his weakness, Gideon fought with lethal skill and strength, spinning his sword around his combatant's in a blur of motion. The man's blade went flying, landing with finality on the grasses beyond his reach, as Gideon ended the battle, stabbing his sword through the soldier's neck. The man's eyes bugged, mouth gaping with a gurgle, as the blade was plunged to the hilt, nearly decapitating him, before he ripped it out.

Stomach heaving, Fiadh retched, spitting foulness into the grasses. She heard Gideon panting as he made his way to her. Turning her head, she took in his bloodied sword and pronounced limp, but despite the toll the fight had taken, she saw pride in his face.

Reaching his hand toward her, he said, "More soldiers will come. We must leave. Now."

She glanced at the woods, wanting their safety, yet fearful that it wouldn't be enough, and then back at him. His hand looked strong and steady as he held it out to her. Reaching forward, she clasped his fingers and stood on trembling legs.

Sensing the indecision in her thoughts, he said, "They will never stop searching for you."

He was right. The peacefulness of the past was gone. Nodding, Fiadh bent and picked up her pack with hands that shook.

"Let us put as much distance between Dorcha Wood and ourselves as we can and hope Darragh's men don't track us."

They slowly made their way toward the border of Darragh's fiefdom as the sun traversed the sky, their lagging pace making Gideon anxious. Frequent glances behind them revealed nothing, but he was on edge, waiting for a contingent of Darragh's men to come crashing down upon them. When they didn't come, he felt no relief, only a foreboding sense that danger was near. He just couldn't see it. Fiadh appeared oblivious, or perhaps it was shock at the swift and brutal attack of the scout who had found them. She trudged along, strain marring the features of her face.

As late afternoon sunlight broke through the clouds,

Gideon heard the shouts he'd been waiting for. Springing into action, he yanked Fiadh out of the open space they had been traveling and into the shelter of trees, shoving her to the ground behind a large oak.

"Stay hidden."

She nodded, horror flooding her face, as the sound of men's yells grew louder. Gideon threw his pack on the ground at her feet and ran, leg dragging slightly, to the edge of the tree line where he could surprise the soldiers as they came by. Cocking his head, he listened, frowning when he heard screams and the shrill whinnies of horses. Minutes passed, and the shouts grew fainter and then stopped. His sword began to waver, and he poked his head out, straining to hear anything more, but all was silent. What had become of them? Shaking his head, he trotted back to Fiadh, pulling her trembling form up and threading her arms through the straps of her pack while she stood like a lost child.

"We will wait a few more minutes. If they don't show themselves, we leave."

She looked at him with wide eyes. "I heard screaming."

"Aye."

"What were they screaming about?"

"I don't know and have no wish to find out," he said grimly.

The soldiers never came. They set off for the east with renewed purpose, eager to get as far from Darragh's reach as possible. Time and distance passed as frayed nerves and overexertion took their toll. Fiadh longed for a horse, but Gideon was averse to the idea when she broached the subject, though they had seen a lonely farmstead in the distance that may have been accommodating. When she prodded him about it, he brushed off the request as too risky being so close to Felmore. Fiadh gave up with a few mumbled complaints, and they carried on.

Only once did they cross paths with anyone, and those souls looked to have come from the north. From a copse of trees, they watched a knight in full battle gear pass by them in a blur of hooves and clanking metal armor on his way toward Felmore, barely glancing at the pair as he rode past. Behind him came his squire, leading a massive warhorse and what looked to be a servant riding a swaybacked gelding with a mule tied to the saddle and loaded with supplies. Gideon stopped, watching their rapid progress, his brow creasing until they were little more than tiny dots in the distance.

"Gideon?" she asked, touching his arm. "Is there something amiss?"

He shook his head. "I had simply hoped for a word, but it matters not."

CHAPTER TWENTY

They stopped in the early evening. Fiadh's entire body felt wrung out, every muscle aching at the abuse of such a long, stressful journey. She couldn't imagine how Gideon felt and took a hard look at her companion. His shoulders slumped, drooping the moment he sat with a groan and dumped his burden onto the ground. Hands hanging limply on his knees, he stared beneath his feet, grumbling to himself too softly for her to hear. Taking furtive glances at him, she unpacked a small meal and spread it on a coarse linen cloth. Tearing off a hunk of dark bread riddled with nuts, she held it out to him.

"You need to eat."

Looking up, he glanced at her offering and took it with a shaky hand, bringing the bread to his mouth. Gideon's jaw worked sluggishly as he chewed his food. Even his teeth ached with weariness as they ground the thick bread into something he could swallow. And his legs? They had become useless things that wouldn't hold his weight if he dared attempt standing.

Fiadh sat, legs tucked under her dress, a handsbreadth from him, gnawing on the end of the loaf. She looked so small—shoulders hunched against the chill. Watching her reinforced the rightness of his choice to take her with him. Feeling his gaze, Fiadh turned her head. "What is it?"

Gideon reached for the leather flask filled with watered wine and took a deep swallow before replying. "I am glad you have come with me. It was the right choice."

She smiled. "Aye. I suppose it was."

"You have doubt?"

"Not doubt. Not after today. But I worry if this is the right path," she said quietly, peering toward the west as though she could see glimpses of Dorcha Wood, but it was too far away now and would only exist in her memories. That was a bitter pill.

"Change is hard," Gideon told her, "but my people will welcome you and, in time, Belfirth will feel like your true home."

"Think you?"

"Aye. I do."

Fiadh nodded but said nothing. Her body felt strange. Dull. Empty. Even the animals she sensed around her, watching the interlopers, seemed fuzzy, as though the impressions she felt from their minds were muted. Perhaps she was just tired, Fiadh thought, letting her body relax as every ache and pain made itself known. The light faded as the sun dipped below the horizon, inviting Mother Moon to bathe the land in her brilliance. Together, they had built a small fire and laid pallets on the hard earth, foot-to-foot, next to the warmth. Eyes trained to the sky, Fiadh watched the stars slowly reveal themselves, smattering the darkness with speckles of light. She listened to Gideon's even breathing, marking the moment when he drifted into a deep sleep.

Rising slowly, she walked a few hundred paces from the light of the fire and perched herself on a large boulder. Wrapping her arms around her knees, Fiadh dropped her head and let the tears come, embracing the wrenching sadness she had kept at bay throughout their journey. Quiet sobs wracked her body, shoulders shaking with the force of them, but eventually, the grief waned, replaced with grim acceptance. Wiping her face on the edge of her shawl, one her mother had often worn, she looked up at the moon. Its pale face looked back at her, cleansing her in its light.

Raising her arms, palms up, Fiadh tilted her head, the moon's luminance bathing her features. As she had done countless times before in the secrecy of Dorcha Wood, far from Mother's worry, Fiadh sent pulses of thought into the ether, directing them upward, beyond the skyline and clouds, to Danu herself. But fear tinged her thoughts as she sent them out, rooted in the worry that being away from the forest would somehow keep her from reaching the Great Mother. Does Danu still live in the world of men? She wondered. Or had she abandoned them? Minutes passed, and Fiadh's worry became anxiety. It had never been so silent. Was she beyond the Great Mother's consciousness?

A soft sigh of relief spilled from her lips when she felt the moment her thoughts were caught, like a fly in the sticky web of a spider. A being who had been part of Fiadh's life since she had any awareness of such things snagged them from the void, tenderly cradled and considered them. It was a forbidden connection from her mother's perspective, one she had tried to squelch in some enigmatic bid to keep

Fiadh from her natural tendencies. But some pulls are too powerful to resist, some curiosities worth seeking out. And so, she had secreted them from her only family. And they had grown, in depth and scope, becoming part of the rhythm of her life. But they were also what separated her from others. She understood that within Riona's warnings and unspoken worry was the knowledge that Fiadh's connection to the unseen and forbidden was an aberration that others would not tolerate.

With a whisper, Fiadh spoke. "Great Mother, I am here." She paused, knowing there would be no verbal response, but experience had taught her to listen with more than her ears. After a few moments, a soft breeze swept by, freeing tendrils of her hair that tickled her face before the wind curled around her body in an embrace. Fiadh smiled, closing her eyes briefly as she opened her heart and mind to a presence that felt as familiar as her own mother's arms. Minutes passed, the gentle rustle of her dress the only sound, flapping in the quiet as the air stroked her skin, causing the flesh on her arms to pebble. Infused in every pass of the currents, was a smell, sweet with undertones of a foreign spice. She only encountered such scents at times like these and had often wondered at their origin. When the winds died down to feathery touches, she gave voice to the words and feelings which had plagued her with every step she took away from her home. *I feel untethered. Dorcha Wood is leagues away... everything I know... Mother is gone. They took her from me... they took my freedom. And... I'm... being hunted.*

The air stirred in a tiny vortex just beyond the rock she sat upon, lifting up debris in angry fits before settling with a sigh of fallen dirt. Fiadh nodded, sensing the anger and grief. *I couldn't stop them. I couldn't stop any of this. And now… now I'm caught up in someone else's fate, and I don't know if I belong entwined with it.* She paused, a lump forming in her throat. *I fear what the future could bring. I fear what lies behind me.* She thought for a moment, then swallowed past the knot in her neck, voicing her deepest worry. *I'm afraid that he will learn to resent my gifts and twist them into something ugly and evil. Would he lock me away?* Her hands clenched as awful thoughts coursed through her mind, interspersed with images, sounds, and smells that made her heart ache and anger boil. *Would he burn me, marking me as an elven witch like they did my mother?*

Movements of air swept around her, hugging her in their invisible grip, sweeping across her lips and cheeks with loving touches. Fiadh forced her mind to go blank and just feel. She longed to hear some meaning in the currents of wind, some semblance of a voice that would quell her worry and guide her fate. But, as always, there was only a mere presence lovingly enfolding her, leaving her to interpret a deeper meaning, if there was any.

CHAPTER TWENTY-ONE

"My lord," the soldier said, kneeling at Darragh's feet as he sat upon the dais in the great hall, "we have found evidence of your men at the edge of Dorcha Wood, and… the body of Iasan."

Darragh rose slowly, his velvet tunic hanging loosely on his thin frame. To a stranger, he would appear frail, but his men knew that beneath that wiry form were muscles of steel and an iron will to guide them. Smoothing his hand over the softness of the fabric to slow the anger which had begun to smolder, Darragh asked, "Iasan is dead?"

"Aye, he and his mount were slain."

"The witch's daughter lives," Darragh muttered.

"My lord?" the soldier asked.

"How did he die? Did you find evidence of elven sorcery?"

Shaking his head, the soldier said, "Iasan was killed in a skirmish, my lord. His wounds were those of a sword."

"Attacked by a man?" Darragh asked, surprised.

"Or a contingent of men," he said. "We found his body in the eastern meadow outside the forest. Donal sent troops to follow their tracks and expects word soon."

Darragh stroked his chin. If not the witch's daughter, then who? A name floated through his mind, and his hand froze. Lord Crommack? Could that old man be seeking vengeance for his daughter's death after all these years? Darragh had told his late wife's father that she had died of an augue, and he had seemed to accept the story at the time. Though, over the years the old lord had sent men to make inquiries, and those who came looked upon Darragh with suspicion. What if word of his mother's foul deeds had finally traveled to Lord Crommack's ears? The man could have sent scouts to take stock of his troops and run into Iasan, killing him to keep their presence a secret. In days, he could amass an army and march on Felmore.

Darragh turned to the soldier. "Tell me of the tracks."

"They looked fresh, and were those of two men on foot. I would assume their mounts were tethered somewhere nearby."

Only two? They would be easily dispatched. A feral smile split Darragh's face as worry over an aging lord going to war against him faded, and desire for Riona's daughter resurfaced. "And what of my men? What of Jarvis, Hammish, and Marcas?"

"Nowhere to be found, my lord."

"Did you scour Dorcha Wood in search of them, Conor?" Darragh asked, the whisper of metal filling the hall as he drew his sword.

Conor shook his head. "Nay, my lord. I wanted to

inform you posthaste to learn your wishes before we seek them out."

"Hm," Darragh said, causing the soldier to gulp. "What was found?"

Conor glanced up, then cast his eyes down, rather than meet the steely gaze boring into him. "We found naught but the tack from three mounts buried under leaves and branches just inside the woods, not far from Iasan's body."

"I see," Darragh said, beginning to pace. "Yet, you did not search the forest for their whereabouts?"

Conor's neck bobbed as he swallowed hard, fear coursing through his veins so violently he imagined his lord could smell it. "A few of the men think they may have been eaten by one of those *things* that roam the wood, like they done to the others," Conor explained, remembering the remains that had been found of the soldiers who had gone into Dorcha Wood on some errand for their lord. He had seen what was left of them, the mangled armor and bits of cloth, all coated in dried blood. "Mayhap they were taken and are being held in the woods, and you had the right of it, my lord... perhaps another witch lives there still."

Darragh's eyebrow rose. "You sound like a frightened woman," he said, lowering his sword. Connor let out a rush of breath, his shoulders losing some of the tension that held them rigid as he delivered his news. Darragh smirked. "You think you have escaped my ire, Conor?"

"Nay, my lord. I would never presume such."

"Good," Darragh said, patting the man on his head as though he were one of the hounds lounging in huge snoring lumps about the room. If the witch's daughter lived in those woods, he would seek her out himself and bring her to his mother. She would bathe in the girl's blood, and he would be there to hear the squeals of terror and pain. And for him? He would ensure Haegna worked her dark magic and used it to give him whatever power that witch held. "If my men are found unharmed, they will be made an example of. And if they are discovered to be under some witch's spell, we will free them and burn her like we did the other."

Conor's eyes darted to Darragh. "I await your will, my lord."

Tapping the tip of his sword on the corner of one of six large tables, Darragh thought over what Conor had said, flipping back to the exchange he'd had with his mother. According to Haegna, his men were beyond her sight, which he supposed could mean death, but his mother hadn't known the witch lived. And if there were a daughter, Haegna had been blind to that, too.

Of course, Darragh realized a search might be futile. Even if her mother had had help from the villagers, the likelihood of the girl having survived all this time was slim. But, what if? A cruel smile lifted his mouth. As his mother had told him, there was one who could lead him to his men. Xander could also foresee his future and had more power than a mere girl. Perhaps it was time to heed those words and capture the mage.

Studying the man who remained kneeling, Darragh's lip curled. He had no tolerance for the fear radiating off his soldier, a superstitious man whose cowardice left him weak and vulnerable. Had he not shown, in the village on the borders of that forest, that his power was greater? He'd taken the whore of Dorcha Wood, the witch folk claimed was under its protection, and slain her right there in full view of all. And what had happened? Nothing. Had he been cast down? Torn apart by ravenous beasts? Cursed with disease? Nay. She'd burned, and he'd laughed and ridden home to wine and venison. Glancing at the sword gripped in his hand, a cruel smile spread across his face.

"Conor," he called out, "are men still in the eastern meadow or were they all sent to track down those who murdered Iasan?"

"A small contingent was left as a precaution, should your guardsmen seek to flee from a hiding place within the wood."

"Then," he crooned, "it appears I have no need of you."

"My lord?" Conor asked, turning his head to see Darragh's sword coming toward him, the blade piercing his eye and sinking into his skull with a sickening crunch. The hounds, smelling blood, sat up, tails wagging.

"Come, my pets," Darragh said, waving his hand. "Feast."

Surrounded by ten men, Darragh thundered into the meadow atop his warhorse, Necromancer, a beast as black as his master's soul and with a temperament to match. The soldiers sprang to attention at the sight of their lord, noting the absence of Conor and needing little imagination to wonder at it. Darragh stopped at the corpse of Iasan, noting the man's head was nearly severed from his body. No woman did this, he thought. Worry over Lord Crommack's intentions, should it be his men who did this, flared again. He ground his teeth, seething, then turned a baleful glare at the woods. If the girl lived, he must have her. With the power his mother thought ran through her veins, he could harness it and use it to fight against Lord Crommack's army should he choose to go to war over the death of his sniveling daughter. Eager to begin, Darragh barked orders to his men, and, as one, they spread out, entering a forest they feared almost as much as the man who rode at their backs, sword at the ready.

As the heavily armored men crossed from the meadow to the forest, trees awakened and closed in. Trunks bent in strange contortions as branches stretched outward, snagging on the faces and forms of men who stared wide-eyed at a forest that appeared sentient. Yelps of pain and fear echoed through the unnatural quiet, followed by shouts from Darragh as he hacked at limbs that reached for him. The deeper the troops traveled, the darker the forest became, as though day had turned to dusk. Men whispered, heads whipping to and from dark recesses that could hide all manner of nightmarish creatures waiting to tear them apart. If not for the man who herded them like lambs to the slaughter, they would have bolted. But the threat of Darragh's blade kept them moving even as Dorcha Wood sought to force them out.

A short time later, a shrill whistle rang out, echoing through the forest. Darragh kicked Necromancer into a gallop and tore through the woods, scattering birds and small animals in his wake as he chased down the source of the sound. Through a break in the trees came the shouts of men, and Darragh followed it, his mouth watering with bloodlust. Necromancer burst into the clearing just beyond a tiny hut, scattering his men who leaped out of the range of the horse's deadly hooves. Darragh yanked on the reins, his mount rearing with a loud whinny, before hopping out of the saddle and landing on the ground with a hard thump. Stalking toward his captain, a man who had been a youth in his father's time, Darragh asked, "Have you found them?"

"Nay, my lord," Donal said, "but they may have been here. It looks as though it was abandoned not long ago."

Lord Darragh stalked forward, grim and determined, pulling open the door with such force it ripped from its hinges, hanging limply from the frame. With men at his back, he entered, sword drawn. It was a small space littered with herbs that spoke of witchery suspended from the ceiling and scant furniture. Stepping fully into the dim hut, he poked at the fireplace, stirring the tip of his sword through the ashes, searching for warm coals. Finding none, Darragh sifted through the meager offerings left behind by whoever lived here. Reaching into a basket, he pulled out a dress, green and worn but sturdy enough to see more years of use. Buried beneath was more clothing, all aged but well cared for. He spun in a slow circle, suspicions confirmed.

"This is where the witch lived."

Donal looked around the hut. "Witch?"

"That Aos Sí whore we burned!" Darragh shouted, his fist clenching around the dress still hanging from his hand.

Donal grunted, taking in the evidence of a woman who dabbled in herbs and all manner of things. Who knew what she did as she blended them into noxious salves and infusions, muttering dark spells as her mortar and pestle ground them into dust?

"My spies tell me she once had a daughter," Darragh muttered, casting about for evidence of the girl.

"I haven't seen a girl, my lord, or any signs of one."

"Hm," Darragh said, crouching to look at an odd depression in the ground close to the hearth, as though someone had slept in the space, though only a lone pallet rested against a rough wall. "If there is a daughter, she will be on her own… helpless. If she exists, I want her found." He told his captain, wetting his lips at the notion of having the girl at his mercy.

A shudder ran down his captain's spine as he imagined what his master would do to the poor girl should she be found. He had a daughter of his own, whom he kept far from his lord's eye. Odious scenarios bloomed in his mind, suddenly fragmented as a sound reverberated through the forest unlike any he had heard before. Part howl. Part growl. It echoed, joined by more alien voices until the entire hut was surrounded by it.

"No wolf makes that noise," Donal whispered, his face turning white. Darragh cocked his head, listening, fear coursing through his veins alongside hate for such a feeling.

From beyond the threshold of the hut, a soldier cried out, "Cù-Sìth! Cù-Sìth are coming!"

Men sprang into action. Donal grabbed his lord, hauling him away from that evil place, out the door, and into an afternoon which grew dimmer with every ragged breath. The howling, if you could call it that, continued in a deluge of haunting sound, growing louder as soldiers raced from the small clearing, tearing through the forest as they choked on screams of terror. Darragh let himself be pulled along in the strong grip of his captain, his mind filled with stories his mother had fed him in the darkness, horrifying tales of vicious beasts who tore unwary men to pieces should they find themselves in a Cù-Sìth's path.

Clambering onto Necromancer's back, Darragh looked around, panic flooding his mind as the voices of the Cù-Sìth multiplied. Digging his heels into the horse's sides, he bolted into the forest, turning back only once to see massive shadows coalescing in the clearing he had departed.

CHAPTER TWENTY-TWO

The following day took Fiadh and Gideon farther from Dorcha Wood, the leagues they traveled, and the open spaces wearing on her. She felt exposed. Gone were the hundreds of voices that filled her mind as she reached out toward the animals of her home. Here, the wildlife felt separate, as though their minds were on a frequency she couldn't access. If she focused, Fiadh could sense them and get a response, but it was different. She felt weak. Drained. And with the growing distance came a deep longing to return, so fierce her feet would find themselves tangled as though a tether pulled at her from where they had come, back home. Each step became a battle, and soon Fiadh called a halt to their progress.

"Gideon, I must stop."

He turned toward her, setting his burden on the ground against the rock she sat upon. "Do you need to rest?"

"I cannot go on."

Gideon nodded. "It has been a grueling day. I'm sorry I have pushed you too far."

"It isn't the distance." Truthfully, they had traveled less today than the day before, their pace slowing as walking took its toll on both of them.

Fiadh dreaded telling Gideon what was in her heart, but there was no denying it. Her mind was consumed with thoughts of the woods, and she was not herself here, so far from them. It was as though the forest itself had become an entity that reached for her through the ground with tentacles of purpose, tugging at her feet and will, wearing her down until all she could do was submit. Part of her wanted to succumb to it, to leave this foreign world and return to her own.

Taking a deep breath, Fiadh blurted, "This feels wrong." He looked at her, confused. "Leaving feels wrong." Gideon stared, dumbfounded. "I'm sorry," she said, casting her eyes to the side. "Dorcha Wood is my home. It's where I belong."

"What?" he asked, incredulous.

"I want to go home."

Gideon's face darkened. She hadn't noted that look before, and it made him ugly. "You are not returning to that evil place."

Fiadh recoiled. Evil? Since when had her home become something evil?

"You will stay with me." She stepped back, shaking her head. "Fiadh, it's not safe to return. You saw what they did to your mother. You've seen them coming for *you*!" he thundered.

He took a few long strides, grumbling, before turning the full force of his ire at her. "And that day in the woods, don't tell me it was the blood of a deer on your clothes. They found you, didn't they?" She sat, mute. "Didn't they?" Fiadh flinched. "They will come for you. They will *never* stop coming for you."

"This doesn't feel right. *I* don't feel right!" she shouted.

Gideon sighed, pinching the bridge of his nose. "What happened to you isn't fair. But it happened. There is no changing it. No going back." He paused, then added, "I know you're scared."

She looked up at him and saw compassion beneath the irritation that had masked it. It *was* fear she felt. Fear and something more, but how could she explain it?

He knelt at her feet. "You must look forward now, to a new life. Don't let the past take hold of you and keep you from your future."

Gideon extended his arms, holding them open in invitation. She balked for a moment, then leaned forward, and he embraced her. The heat of his chest sank into her, past her anxiety and longing, like an arrow to her heart. Fiadh's head tucked itself beneath his chin, and he tenderly strengthened his hold, encompassing her in such a way his warmth radiated throughout her body, easing her tense muscles as his hands began a rhythmic motion on her back. They felt so much like her mother's hands in those moments that a soft cry broke from her lips. He hummed a strange tune in her ear as she released the grief and worry that had been smothered throughout the leagues they had traveled. It tore from her in waves, her chest shuddering with it. Fiadh let it go like venom from a wound.

When her tears became hiccups and quaky breaths, Gideon broke the silence. "I cannot let you go back, Fiadh." His hands ran up and down her arms as her cheek remained pressed to his heart. "There are dangerous people in this world. You have seen their work. If you were to return, it would surely be to your death, and I can't stomach that certainty."

"You don't know that would happen," she mumbled wetly.

He sighed. "You know nothing of the world beyond your wood." She reared back with a flash of anger. Pressing a finger to her lips, he silenced her protest. "All your life, your good mother, Riona, kept you safe and hidden from the ugliness of it." Fiadh cast her glance aside, the image of Mother and her many warnings filling her mind. "Now, that cruelty has found you."

"You can't know what harm may come to me if I returned," she argued half-heartedly.

Gideon looked at her, a pained expression causing the skin around his eyes to crinkle. "It would be folly to give in to your fears of a new life and go back." She looked away, and he curled a finger under her chin, gently pulling her back toward his face. "Do you think I can't understand your longing? To be where you spent such happy days in safety. I know the feelings that are tugging at you. I have felt them too."

"Gideon, I feel lost and not myself," her voice cracked, "as though I am floating on some strange wind that is carrying me away from who I am and what I love."

"That is how I felt as I was under your fine care. It is the truth I feel some of it still, as I am unable to recall the events that led me to you. But Fiadh, that same fate has brought us together. Can you not feel the rightness of it?"

His question flooded her, sinking into her mind before winding its way into her heart, where it bloomed with meaning. She clutched her chest, afraid of what it might signify to reach out and take what he had offered in that small statement.

Gideon's fingers traced her face, learning the dips and planes, the curves and softness. "Will you stay with me?" he whispered, letting moments pass as she listened to the words with more than her ears. "Stay by my side, meet my family and my people. Walk with me and see where it leads you, and, if after you have a taste of what could be, you decide you must return, I will escort you myself."

Fiadh's eyes pooled. Her will fought her heart, but the battle was brief. "All right."

Gideon smiled, leaning down to press his lips against hers. She felt the smoothness as his hands sank into her hair, cupping the back of her skull, his fingers brushing against the tips of her scarred ears. Tilting his head, he parted his mouth and touched his tongue to her lips. Fiadh tried to pull away at the strangeness of it, but his gentle grip held her fast and, slowly, she opened to his questing and felt the sweet invasion in her mouth. Sensations rippled through her stomach, unlike any she had felt before, and it left her trembling and cautious of the feelings he had stirred.

Pulling away, Gideon chastely kissed her mouth again, then the tip of her nose and her forehead, before pressing his cheek against her hairline and murmuring, "I was destined to find you."

Fiadh nodded, her head bumping his jaw. "Perhaps it is time to begin again."

Breathing in her scent, he closed his eyes, feeling all of the ways being with Fiadh felt right. She was meant to save him, and he was meant to save her, and he believed those events were the first tentative steps in a new future. Rubbing her arms briskly, he asked, "Shall we continue?"

"Aye," she replied, picking up the basket she had slung to the ground when they stopped.

He did the same, taking her hand and kissing the tips of each finger before striking out for the east. As they walked, he worked to lighten the mood engaging her in storytelling of their youth. They passed the hours sharing everything from the humorous to the heartfelt, though it became clear Fiadh's experiences were tainted with a longing to be with others her age.

After Gideon shared a recollection of his first hunt and the pride Lord Ross had felt at that rite of passage, he turned to her. Fiadh sensed the question coming before he asked and was ready when she heard him say, "What of your father? You mentioned he and your brother died when you were small."

Fiadh's stride slowed, her mind taking her back to memories that had grown dim with time. What she recalled weren't her remembrances. They were those her mother had instilled throughout the years, shared so many times the stories had grown in depth and imagery. Riona had kept her father and brother alive with those retellings, and now she had to maintain their memory on her own.

"Our home hadn't always been in Dorcha Wood, though that is all I remember. My family had lived in Felmore, on a remote farm close to the forest, Mother told me. Father raised sheep, selling the wool at market each spring. It was a small flock, to begin with, but had been thinned by disease and theft over numerous seasons before he died. My brother, Callum, was my twin."

Gideon sucked in a quick breath of surprise.

Fiadh smiled sadly. "Mother said if not for our clothing, she couldn't tell us apart. Callum had long dark hair Mother refused to cut, and pale skin, like me. He was truly Father's shadow, following him into the fields or the village."

She set down her basket and sat against a tree, Gideon joining her. "Mother said the day Callum and Father died, he and I were nearly three. She and Father had sheared the sheep, and he was taking the fleece to market. Callum, never one to be left behind, joined him while Mother and I remained home. A violent storm swept through the village, felling a tree that crushed them both."

"It saddens me to learn you had to go through such tragedy when you were so young."

Fiadh nodded. "Mother took me to Dorcha Wood after that. I think she was afraid of living as a widow in the village." Fiadh paused, fiddling with her hands. "The forest is all I know. For me, the fear of it makes no sense. It has… had… been our haven. It is out here, the world beyond the woods, that I fear."

"I am truly sorry you were forced to leave it in such a way." He leaned forward, pulling her closer, so her hip rested against his. She could feel his warmth seep through her clothing.

"I wish I could change it."

"I know." Gideon kissed her head, trailing his lips along her hairline before gently taking her chin and turning it toward his mouth, where he captured her lips. Her heart beat rapidly, thundering in her ears as blood rushed through her body, and she wondered if he could hear it. When he pulled away, she saw his chest heaving and knew he was just as affected as she. Taking her hand, he traced his fingers along the fine lines of her palm. "You have captured my heart, Fiadh."

Her lips trembled in a small smile as color rushed to her cheeks. It was so much so fast and, while she couldn't deny the feelings he elicited, she was unwilling to surrender fully. He didn't know who she was, not entirely. How could he love her when he didn't truly know her? And if he did, would he turn her away?

The quiet was shattered as a small contingent of soldiers, and their entourage rode into view, their horses lathered in foamy sweat as their riders urged them onward at breakneck speeds. Gideon grabbed her roughly, and tucked her behind his back. She poked her head around his broad chest and immediately wished she hadn't. Her hands clenched as she saw one of the men swing his reins in a vicious arc, whipping his horse's side with such force blood splattered from wounds that had likely been inflicted throughout their journey. She tried to move past Gideon, ready to throw herself in front of the riders to stop the abuse, but he yanked her back. "Let them pass. There is bloodlust in their eyes."

She looked at the soldiers' faces, grim and hard, mouths twisted with ugly purpose. Gideon was right. They were beyond reason, set upon some task that would brook no interference. Sadness swamped her as she watched the poor horse receive another round of cruel whipping. Reaching out her mind, she tried to touch his, but there was only a dull response, as though his mind was too strange for her to feel. Fiadh clenched her fists and focused, visualizing his form, trying to feel his racing heart and the beat of his hooves on the ground. After untold moments, more than it had ever taken before, she felt him flinch at her intrusion, and she followed that reaction into his mind. Fiadh reached into him, calming him as much as she could, sending warm emotions rather than the harsh misery he received with every lash. The feelings wouldn't last, but perhaps they would be a welcome respite.

They sheltered against a tree, hidden from view until the sound of hooves pounding into the earth was gone. Gideon stood and looked at where they had just been swallowed into the rolling hills, noting the direction they traveled. It frustrated him that he hadn't been able to make out the banners they rode under. "The other rider had gone the same way. Toward Felmore."

Fiadh followed his gaze. "Perhaps they go to see Lord Darragh."

"Aye, but why such haste?" To that, she had no answer. He let out a long sigh. "I would likely know the reason if I were at Belfirth. Let us move on." Swinging their heavy packs onto their backs, they resumed their journey, but Fiadh caught Gideon contemplating where the riders had gone, an expression of worry on his face.

CHAPTER TWENTY-THREE

$\mathcal{A}$s hours passed, Gideon's limp became more pronounced. Eventually, he stopped, slinging his burden to the ground before hobbling to a large boulder where he sat with a loud moan, stretching his leg while he kneaded the muscles.

"You are pushing yourself too hard," Fiadh scolded.

"Aye, I know it, but I am eager to get us to the safety of my castle. While I feel we are safe from Darragh's men, it is not unheard of for marauders to be about attacking travelers. We are fortunate to have only encountered soldiers." Fiadh looked around, startled by the idea. He chuckled. "Be at ease, I have been vigilant, and I am not so weak I couldn't brandish my sword and give them a fight. Though you have none to compare me to, I am quite skilled with a blade and have well-earned my reputation."

Fiadh cocked an eyebrow. "Oh? Tell me a tale of your prowess then," she said while unpacking a few supplies for the evening.

"A story of one of my feats?" He smirked, thinking for a

few moments. "When I was but a lad of eight and Doran just five summers, we came upon a beast that had found itself in the kitchen gardens. Rather than calling for the guard, or my father, I decided we must oust this intruder ourselves and find us heroes." Fiadh rolled her eyes and clucked her tongue. "Running to the armory, I took a sword and shield, dropping the latter when its weight became too much. Deciding I required no defense, I left the shield and stalked into the garden, with Doran at my heels. Naught but a few paces from where we had left it, was the creature, a wiry thing snuffling through the lettuces. Certain it would turn bloodthirsty the moment it caught our scent, I raised the sword and let out my most ferocious battle cry.

Upon hearing my terrifying yell, it lifted its head, its mouth dripping with the carcasses of defenseless herbs and greens, and snorted at us, stalking forward with a menacing grunt. Doran ran, leaving me to deal with the beast alone, and I would have, if not for the trowel some careless soul had left rooted in the soil just behind me. Tripping, I fell with a cry, my sword flying from my arms and falling useless in a muddy patch of dirt. The beast came for me then. I looked into its evil stare and knew my life would end, but, being incredibly brave, I rallied my courage and sprang to my feet, startling the monster. I charged it with a tremendous roar and sent it squealing into the forest from which it had come. Having found Doran sobbing in the great hall, my mother came running into the garden at that moment and found me standing, with my hands on my hips and my chest puffed with pride. And that was how my legendary reputation as a fearless warrior began."

"And the beast?" she asked.

"I am happy to say the pig never returned to our gardens," Gideon said, cocking his eyebrow and smirking.

Fiadh burst out laughing. "Gideon, savior of herbs and lettuces!"

"Aye, my reputation proceeds me. Now, tell me one of your tales. Share something no other has heard before."

A story of the Cù-Sìth popped into her mind, but she quickly set it aside. That was a secret that would remain as such. "Hm. Let me think," she cocked her head. "Ah, I have one you may find entertaining." Fiadh proceeded to regale him with a story of a litter of skunks whose mother had died, leaving them orphans. "When I brought them home, smuggled in my shawl, Mother had no inkling of what I was about for all of a few moments. It was their soft squeals and purrs reaching her sharp ears which alerted her, and she turned on me, a spoon clutched in her hand, as their wriggling bodies spilled from the covering." Fiadh laughed. "Oh, the look on her face when she spied their tiny black and white bodies! Thankfully, she stopped herself before yelling at me, likely realizing doing so would only result in panicking the poor creatures, making a stench no amount of cleaning could ever purge. I pled my case, begging to keep them, and she conceded, but only if I made them a makeshift shelter outside. It was a long span of weeks, but eventually, the babies grew strong enough to be on their own. Of course, Mother always hated it when they came back for a visit, giving an exasperated sigh and scuttling inside with mutters of distaste as I fed them from my hand or stroked their soft fur. Had you stayed longer, you would have seen their offspring, my sweet brood having introduced me to their mates and young a couple of seasons ago."

Fiadh chuckled. "Mother was tolerant of all my creatures, except those. She never could accept their presence, and they knew it, often waddling after her with tails raised if she came too close."

Gideon laughed, picturing this lovely woman rearing such creatures. "It is a wonder Riona didn't have more grey on her head!"

"Aye, I suppose it is," Fiadh snickered.

"In Belfirth, you must share your adventures with my mother. She has always loved animals. If she isn't in the solar or the gardens, my father inevitably finds her in the stables, feeding the horses apples and carrots."

Fiadh smiled. "It is good to hear that we share that affinity."

"Aye," he replied. "Though my father never admitted such, I have always sensed Mother was a bit of a hellion in her youth. I think you and she may have much in common."

"Are you saying I am a trouble-maker?"

"My lady, I'm beginning to think trouble would seek you out for sport!"

Fiadh laughed but couldn't deny the idea, especially in light of recent events. "I suppose there is some truth in that, though I have never sought it out."

Gideon cocked a brow. "Oh? Why does that sound like a falsehood on your tongue?"

Blushing, she smacked his arm. "As you said, trouble finds *me* whether I will it or not."

He nodded. "True enough. Let us hope it has lost you for good."

She looked wistful as her gaze took in their surroundings. "Mother and I used to jest like this. She had a great wit." Gideon smiled sadly as he listened. "I miss her."

"I know."

"Do you think your people will accept me? An outsider?"

The question took him by surprise, and he cocked his head. "As with anything, there will be an adjustment, but they will. I promise." Gideon took her hand. "Fiadh, I know you worry you will be an outcast, but those worries are for naught. I will protect you from any wagging tongues. You will be safe."

She nodded. "I know you will do all you can, but I am from Dorcha Wood. Do you not think your people will be riddled with suspicion when they hear?"

"Nay, for we won't tell them."

"I see," she said, hurt at the confirmation of his prejudice. "That is probably best, though I am not ashamed of my home."

"And you have no need to be, Fiadh. But these are simple folk who have grown up hearing stories of that place. Some still believe the mythological Cù-Sìth roam those woods, murdering the unwary!"

Fiadh made a face. "Aye, I am sure many believe such tales."

"A great number of my people died in the elven wars, and stories of those dark days have been passed down from old to young, year after year. That history lives within Belfirth folk," Gideon said. "To speak of Dorcha Wood could invite old hatreds. It would be easier to tell them you are of Felmore. It's true, after all. Felmore is the place of your birth. Let us keep it at that. Perhaps, in time, you can tell the people of your life in Dorcha Wood, once they know you, have taken your measure, and you have become part of them."

Fiadh couldn't argue with his reasoning. After what she had witnessed, there was no denying how twisted the minds of some could become, and she had no desire to be at the receiving end of such willful hatred. But to have Gideon say the words made her realize she was right to keep things from him. He would likely see her as a monster if he knew, and that knowledge made her heart ache.

"I can do that," she told him. "But I have a deep love of my home. Of the forest, and all life within it."

"As you should."

Looking away, Fiadh let out a slow breath. "My life has been utterly changed. I don't recognize it anymore."

"I'm sorry. If I had the power to alter it, I would," he paused, "though letting you go would be nigh unto impossible."

She turned toward him, a crooked smile on her face, at odds with the moisture in her eyes. "Would it?"

"Have you no idea what you have done to me?"

She shook her head.

"You have turned me into a besotted pup! Never have I longed for a woman as I long for you. See what you have made of me, my Fiadh?" Gideon flung his arms out. "I was once a warrior of some repute, but now I am no better than those fools minstrels sing of."

"I wouldn't know such songs," she countered. "Perhaps you could sing one to me?"

Gideon chuckled. "If I were to attempt such a thing, birds and all manner of furry things would flee."

Fiadh laughed with him, her emotions fluctuating in the chaos of her life at this moment. But it felt good to laugh, to hear him speak of his feelings for her, though she couldn't say how deeply she returned them. There was too much darkness, too many secrets, in her life right now to give herself fully. And he didn't know her. Not all of who she was. And, maybe, he never would.

Gideon looked at Fiadh. Her radiant green eyes had become calm, the sadness that had made them dull and clouded, having retreated. "I want you by my side, Fiadh. Fate has led me to you, and I am not one to argue with her guiding hand."

"Thank you," Fiadh said softly. But she wondered at his statement. Was he suggesting a marriage in their future? Had she understood that right? The idea felt daunting. So permanent. And wouldn't his family protest such a match? She was a nobody, and he was a noble's son. It could never work, but she had no heart to say anything. Let him believe, just for a moment, that a bright future together was possible. After all, it was a beautiful idea.

"You do know I would never force you to remain with me should my home not suit you in the end," Gideon said.

"You wouldn't?" She teased.

"Well, perhaps I was too hasty." He chuckled. "But, all laughter aside," he said, taking her hand, "the choice of whether to carve out a life with me or not will be yours."

A lump clogged her throat and she swallowed it down. "It's good to hear those words."

"Each one was meant."

Gideon reached for her, a grin curving his lips, as he swooped in to seize her mouth. His lips and tongue brushed against hers. Feeling her body begin to sway under the onslaught of his skilled mouth, Fiadh hooked her arms around his neck, seeking ballast, and let him consume her.

"You are mine," he whispered, nipping gently at her bottom lip. She nodded, overwhelmed by sensations churning in her stomach like wings beating in frantic rhythms. It wasn't an unpleasant feeling. His hands slid down her sides, following the curve of her hips before they paused. Gideon's eyes clenched, and his breathing became an irregular pulse in her ears as he pulled away. "We must stop before I lack the will to."

Fiadh unhooked her arms from around his neck, noting how they trembled before they dropped into her lap like dead things. "You make me feel strange," she said softly.

He traced her lips with his finger. "There is much more I could make you feel, but I won't taint your innocence. If you choose to remain at my side," he purred, "you will experience things you never dreamed possible."

The walls were coming down, one by one, as he spun fantasies in her mind. Slowly, she was letting go of her past and looking toward the future. For the first time since they started on this journey, she had hope.

CHAPTER TWENTY-FOUR

Gideon led Fiadh to a small copse of trees on legs that quivered with each step as the sun began its slow descent. He watched as she dropped her heavy basket and stretched her back, arms reaching for the sky and then swinging from side to side in slow movements, letting blood flow freely, and muscles release their tension. Gideon was almost afraid to sit, unsure if he'd be able to stand again. And his armor? He would have to sleep in it as the idea of removing each piece felt insurmountable. Fiadh sensed his eyes on her and reached for his pack, sliding it from him as he stood, immobile. Digging into the contents, she pulled out the worn blanket he'd been using as bedding and spread it on the ground.

"Take your ease. You have pushed yourself too far today."

"We need a fire," he said, his body lurching toward the trees where wood lay scattered on the ground.

Fiadh snagged his arm, pulling him toward the bedding. "I will tend to that. You must lie down before you fall." He started to grumble but thought better of it and let her push him gently to the ground. With a sigh, he closed his eyes, her soft footfalls receding from his awareness.

Small twigs and branches spilled from Fiadh's arms as she made her way deeper into the trees, scouting for firewood. Bending, she picked up the best of those which had fallen and piled them back into her arms, scanning the forest floor for more. It felt good to be within this small forest, the presence of so much life around her, so much like home, was a balm. In these surroundings, she felt somewhat herself. The sound of wood snapping stopped her progress. She held her breath and focused on the noises around her, listening for any stirring of living things. Turning slowly, she let out a startled gasp. "Krulan!"

Before her stood the leader of the Cù-Sìth, his hulking form a mass of darkness beneath the canopy. *You scared me. Where did you come from?*

I never left.

What?

I have been with you since you left Dorcha Wood.

"Why?" Fiadh asked before realizing she spoke aloud. She looked toward the break in the trees where Gideon dozed, but he didn't stir. *Why have you followed me?*

You left the wood, and I must follow.

That makes no sense, she told him. *Dorcha Wood is your home. You said yourself you could not leave the forest.*

This is Dorcha Wood.

Fiadh glanced around. *What do you mean?*

Dorcha Wood spanned many leagues before men destroyed it. The heart of it remains where you call home, but it is all of this land, though so much has been butchered and burned that its power and strength wane beyond the borders of your home.

Surveying their surroundings, Fiadh tried to imagine the forest having spanned such great distances. It saddened her to think so much had been lost. And she had felt it. Perhaps, Dorcha Wood had somehow shared itself with her very being, and it was only now, when she was far from it, that its loss was recognized. It would explain much she had experienced, though not all. *You are the warden of Erabel, the territory of the Cù-Sìth, are you not?*

I am. Krulan replied, though it had felt as though he would add something more for a moment.

How can you fulfill that role if you're following after me?

Others will protect the kingdom.

Fiadh let out a small huff, bending forward to grab a thick stick. Straightening, she asked, *If you could leave Dorcha Wood all along, why didn't you save my mother?*

She is not our protected.

Fiadh stopped and glared at him. *She should've been. I don't understand why you think I am someone worthy of your protection if she wasn't. Mother was… she was better, kinder, than I could ever be.*

Her character matters not.

Grabbing a stick, Fiadh waved it at him. *Mayhap you need to rethink who it is you deem worthy, Krulan!*

He stood silent under her rebuke and held her stare.

Fine. Do what you will, she snapped and resumed gathering wood. *Why haven't you made yourself known before now?*

Krulan rolled his shoulder in an undulating motion so like a shrug. *I have watched and kept you safe.*

What do you mean, kept me safe?

They tracked you and would have found you had I not intervened.

She grabbed her chest, remembering the screams of men and whinnies of horses as she and Gideon had hidden from Darragh's soldiers. *Did you… did you kill those men?*

Had I not, they would have captured you.

Fiadh's heart raced with what Krulan had said. How many more men had died because of her?

Their deaths are insignificant.

How can you say that? she asked, appalled.

You are my protected. Should your life be in danger, I will rip out the throats of those who seek to harm.

The image his statement conjured flashed in gory brilliance within her mind. Glancing at his teeth, she recalled him ruthlessly tearing through flesh. Remembering made her feel sick. *I hope to never need your aid again. But I… I thank you for protecting me,* she offered, not wanting to offend such a powerful being. *I still don't understand why, though. Come to think of it, I don't understand how you knew of me before our first encounter.*

You are known. Your birth was shared among my brothers and sisters.

But, why? Why would the birth of a human mean anything to your kind? Stories of the Cù-Sìth spun through her mind, those terrible imaginings which kept children in their beds, too afraid to set a toe beyond the covers as the dark of night swallowed their security in its blackness.

Your name was whispered on the wind. We have known of you since that time and been watchful.

Fiadh frowned. *That makes no sense.*

It will. In time.

You know more than what you are telling me, she accused him. The weight of the wood in her arms felt heavy, as though this whole exchange was pressing down on her. She unfolded her arms, letting the bundle of sticks and branches cascade to the pine-needle littered ground in soft thumps. *Why the secrecy?*

It is for me to watch and guard. It is for others to share wisdoms and histories.

Fiadh mumbled her disagreement. It was frustratingly clear she wasn't going to learn anything beyond the limited information Krulan told her. For whatever reason, he would only say so much. But she and Gideon must be close to his land, and then Krulan would return to Dorcha Wood. *Very well. Will you be following me throughout the rest of my journey?*

I will.

And when we arrive, you will return to your home?

Krulan gave a low growl but said nothing.

I wonder what Gideon would say, should he see you? she mused.

I would not give him the chance to utter a sound.

You mean… you would kill him? He tilted his head up in the semblance of a nod. *Why?*

Tales of my kind must not leave the wood. To be seen beyond the forest is forbidden.

That's wrong, Krulan. You can't simply kill someone for having seen you. Fear for Gideon made her heart race.

It is our way.

That doesn't make it right. The sound of Gideon stirring sent a pang of alarm through Fiadh. *I forbid you from hurting him!*

You do not have that power.

It was startling to realize she had two protectors, neither of whom she could control. It was frightening. She swooped down and snatched a large armful of the firewood she had dropped, ignoring the pieces which quickly fell again from her grasp. "Don't hurt him," she whispered harshly before turning her back and walking briskly to their encampment.

I will be with you, Fiadh.

It was the first time he had acknowledged her name. It made her stumble and crane her neck to look at him, but Krulan was already melting into the darkness.

CHAPTER TWENTY-FIVE

Morning brought with it a tangible sense of being watched. It itched between her shoulder blades and ran along her scalp in tingles of awareness. Furtive glances into the woods showed her nothing, but Fiadh knew Krulan was there, watching.

Gideon sensed her unease. "Are you well?"

Fiadh made a face, pulling her eyes away from a small movement in the trees to focus on him. "I'm a bit tired. You? Your wounds?"

He rubbed his leg, working out the muscles which had grown tight during the night. "Well enough. Let us see how the day goes and where the winds of destiny take us."

She nodded, rolling up her blanket before setting it aside and handing Gideon an oatcake. They ate in silence for a time, listening to the sounds of the forest awakening. "Tell me of your home. What does it look like?"

"It sits at the base of Viliock Mountain with the whole of our lands stretching before the stronghold and solid rock at its back." His stare grew wistful, drifting to the horizon.

"Our soil is rich, dark with few stones, though most of Belfirth's wealth is in sheep. The demesne itself has been in my family for more than a hundred years. It is all I have known, and, one day, it will be mine, and I will charge my own son with its endurance."

"It is good to know where you belong."

"You will belong to that land too," he said quietly.

The corners of Fiadh's mouth lifted slightly, and she raised a brow. "Mayhap."

"Mayhap?" Gideon said with an exaggerated gasp. "Are you going to taunt me with your reticence and then leave me in a state of misery?"

"There is some appeal to that," she chuckled.

He scowled. "Ah, you heartless woman. See how you torture me?"

Fiadh laughed, the sound filling the quiet. "I have yet to see your home nor meet your people, and you want me to promise my eternal devotion?"

"Insignificant details," he scoffed.

She rolled her eyes. "You're incorrigible."

"Ah, she finally sees through the chivalry to the man beneath." He snickered, enjoying their banter. There was a marked difference in her demeanor around him, and Gideon relished it, the intimacy and comfort. He could picture spending a lifetime with Fiadh and hoped that one day she would feel the same.

They packed up the remainder of their belongings and set off for the east. As she walked, Fiadh felt Krulan's presence. Quick glances told her he remained unseen, keeping to dense clusters of trees, but her body felt alive with awareness as they trekked across a landscape she had never thought to see. Truth be told, she had never wanted to leave the borders of Dorcha Wood, content to live and die there. Life has a way of pulling us from what we know, she mused, and setting us on a new path. And, if she were being honest, a future with Gideon, a life in a community rather than as a recluse, was becoming more enticing.

On a bluff, a small farm came into view, smoke drifting into the sky. Fiadh stopped and stared. "There is a house over there," she said, pointing.

Gideon followed her finger. "Aye. You will find those who wish to live on their own, though most fear the solitude and risks of being so isolated."

She nodded. "They just want what I had. Freedom."

"Perhaps," he said. "Some who choose that path were indentured servants who wish to work their own land, beholden to no one. I imagine the only time they see another soul is when travelers pass by or if they make their way to festivals or villages to trade. These lands are beyond anyone's borders. And beyond their protection."

Fiadh looked wistfully, a smile curving her mouth.

"Come," he said, tugging her hand.

"What?"

"Let us see if they have a horse we can borrow."

"A horse," she said with a gush of relief. "I will admit my legs and back would appreciate that."

"Hopefully, my natural charm, and a coin or two, will find us with a sturdy mount."

Fiadh smiled, and they made their way to the farmstead.

A middle-aged man greeted them from a small field he had been clearing in preparation for spring planting. The team of oxen he left tethered to the plow bawled loudly, their voices echoing in the pastoral scene. Brushing dirt from his hands and rubbing them nervously, he asked, "Milord, may I be of help?"

"Aye," Gideon replied, giving the man a quick smile. "I am Gideon of Belfirth, and this is my companion, Fiadh of Felmore. We are making our way to my lands and have need of a horse."

The farmer's eyes darted between them, and he fidgeted. "My wife and I lived within your borders before we earned our freedom."

"And a fine home you've made for yourself," Gideon said, putting the man at ease.

His shoulders visibly relaxed. "I have no horse, milord. Only the oxen." He waved his hand at the animals. "May I offer you a small meal instead?"

Fiadh struggled not to show her disappointment as she stood just behind Gideon, feeling self-conscious.

"We would appreciate a meal if you have food to spare," Gideon said.

The man nodded. "I am Owen," he told them, indicating they should follow.

Gideon reached back and took Fiadh's hand, squeezing it, and the three of them made a short trek to Owen's tiny house. Swinging the door open, Owen ushered them inside. The interior was dark, lit by a few candles which guttered from the breeze coming through the doorway as Owen shut them in. A woman with red hair stood at the fireplace, her hand frozen midair, the spoon she clutched dripping sauce onto the dirt floor.

Clearing his throat, Owen said, "Marion, we have visitors who would like a meal."

Marion's mouth worked for a few moments before she collected herself. "Aye, a meal. There is plenty to share. Would you like to sit?"

Owen pulled up the only stools in the home, set them a few paces from the fire's warmth, and then stood awkwardly. "Have you traveled far?" he asked, his voice too loud for the small space.

Gideon nodded. "Aye, we have come a fair distance. From Felmore, actually."

"Have you no horse and squire, milord?"

Chuckling, Gideon said, "It is a sad state we find ourselves in. While we began our journey well enough, we now find ourselves with naught but our feet and the packs on our backs." Fiadh was impressed by how quickly Gideon devised his story.

When no other details were offered, Owen laughed nervously and stalked to his wife. "Is the meal ready?" he asked, poking his finger into the pot and popping it in his mouth with a slurp.

"Aye, husband. Fetch the bowls."

Marion dished out the stew and handed it to them. Fiadh smiled shyly and mumbled a thank you, feeling embarrassed and out of place, as she noted the man and woman weren't eating, likely because there were only two bowls, to begin with.

Between bites, Gideon said, "Have you any news? Any other visitors?"

Owen shifted his weight and looked at his wife. "None that stopped for more than a word."

Gideon cocked his eyebrow. "Aye? When was that?"

"Just two days past, a few riders coming from the north.

They passed through, only stopping to ask if we had seen others."

"They may have been the riders we saw heading to Felmore," Gideon said to Fiadh, who nodded.

"Is there aught amiss, milord?" Owen asked.

"Not that I have heard." Gideon glanced at the doorway, his face creasing with worry.

Marion scuttled closer to Fiadh. "Milady," she said, "is the meal to your liking?"

Fiadh blushed. *A lady?* she mused. *Does she think I'm a lady?* Fumbling for words, Fiadh said, "It is delicious… thank… thank you."

The woman smiled, her chest puffing with pride which her husband echoed. "Marion is a splendid cook."

"Aye, she is that," Gideon said, earning him wide grins from the husband and wife.

Having finished, Fiadh rose and cast about for a place to wash her bowl. "Have you a basin I can wash this in?"

Marion gasped and swooped in to grab the bowl and spoon from Fiadh. "Nay, milady! You sit yourself down and take your ease."

Fiadh sat, feeling as though she had made a social blunder and at a loss as to how to act. These were simple folk, not nobility, yet she had limited experience interacting with anyone and felt clumsy. The realization forced her to recognize how much she had missed living so remotely in Dorcha Wood. Mother had been fine company, but how often had she hid in the shadows and watched village life? How many times had she longed to be part of it? Now, thanks to Gideon, she could be.

Squaring her shoulders, Fiadh sat straighter and listened

as Owen and Gideon chatted about the fall harvest and the farmer's plans for a spring crop. Hearing their easy banter, she saw the title Gideon wore. His mannerisms and speech seemed lordly, or how she imagined lordly to be. Somehow, he had put the couple at ease and spoke with the experience of a man who could navigate any situation with grace rather than the gawkiness she felt.

A longing took hold of her as she sat and watched. Human interaction. This is what she had been missing. This is what a future with the regal man who sat beside her could bring. Something in her shifted and settled into place. Dorcha Wood was her past. And, perhaps, she would return to that special place, but at that moment, she felt a deep longing to reach for a different future. To be part of a bigger world, no matter how daunting that choice may seem. Gideon looked at her, paused mid-sentence, and smiled. She returned it and reached for his hand, seeing a burst of pleasure cross his face. They left a short time later, Fiadh's steps lighter despite the aching in her legs.

CHAPTER TWENTY-SIX

At midday, Gideon's pace quickened as they came upon the edge of a stretch of land with rolling hills and large meadows. Clusters of trees dotted the picturesque countryside, adding variation to the scenery. In the distance, she could see a gathering of birds swooping from the earth to the sky in random dips and whirls. They were large, perhaps a murder of crows, but she was too far away to see them clearly. Fiadh stopped to focus on them, trying to discern their movements and interest. Gideon halted next to her, shading his eyes from the sun's glare that had broken through the mass of clouds that filled the sky.

"Is that the border of your land?" she asked, peering into the distance.

"Nay, it is just beyond those hills," Gideon told her, pointing away from the odd collection of birds.

Pulling her attention from the flock, which suddenly felt ominous, Fiadh said, "Let us move on," unease sweeping through her at the sight of those dark forms in the sky. She began walking in the direction he had pointed and got a few paces from his side before realizing he hadn't moved. "Gideon?" His stare was fixed on the horizon, watching the movements in the sky. "Shall we go on?"

"There is something there. I think… I think we must go there first. There's a familiarity about that swath of land. I can feel memories crawling through my brain."

When he looked at her, Fiadh stepped back. His eyes had gone wild, frantic, in a face that had lost its color. "What is it?"

Gazing into the distance again, he whispered, "I think it may be whatever my mind has shut away from me."

Striking out across the land away from Belfirth, they headed toward the mass of birds that grew in number and size the closer they came, their black bodies becoming a blur of darkness like a storm cloud. Gideon's gait became awkward at the increased pace, his leg seeming to drag the farther they traveled up and down the rolling land, creating a small rut in the grasses. Lips mashed together, he struggled on, the force of his will pushing him beyond his natural endurance. Thoughts of Krulan, wherever he lurked in the peripheral, taunted Fiadh as she waited for Gideon's strength to give out, ready to take his burden should he begin to fall.

The smell hit them first. There is nothing like the odor of death, that rancid permeation in the air which digs into your nostrils until all other scents are masked in its putridity. Long before they crested the hill, Fiadh knew what they would find. A massacre.

Bloated bodies littered the ground in twisted masses, legs and arms bent at awkward angles, while faces, mottled with blackened blood that had collected just below the skin's surface, lay frozen in gruesome masks of agony. Empty eye sockets, whose cavernous stares gazed unseeing, held her fast as though the power of sight still lay buried in their deathly aspects. There were tens of hundreds blanketing ground that had turned black. Her eyes darted among the bodies, wanting to look away but unable to. There are no horses, her mind spluttered. Not one. Her mind felt jumbled as her eyes jumped from one corpse to another. Her head spun. Bodies. Misshapen bodies, thick with rot from days of exposure, mutilated by animals feasting on the carrion for days. It was like the earth itself had spat out this mass of mangled soldiers, and here they lay, skin purpling above pools of stagnant blood.

Nothing moved, save the birds, fat black vultures in numbers that outmatched the corpses they swarmed over. With wings splayed to fend off rivals, they bobbed their heads in threatening postures, hopping from body to body in displays of prowess, fighting for the rotting flesh. Fiadh covered her mouth as stomach acid churned in her gut, threatening to spill from her lips in forceful torrents. She swallowed hard, the movement making her gag. Swinging away from the ghastly scene, she fell to her knees and vomited, taking huge gulps of air when her stomach finally emptied.

Coming back to herself, she swung around, her body too riddled with shock to stand, and stared at Gideon, who stood immobile. She knew without asking that his father and brother lay among the dead. He had watched Doran fall. The nightmares he still screamed in the night had told her as much. But this, this was a slaughter on a colossal scale. This attack was meant to obliterate.

"Gideon?" she called, her voice startling in this deathly landscape. "Gideon?" After a few moments, he turned toward her. He looked haunted. "Gideon, we must leave this place. Whoever did this may come back."

Swinging his stricken gaze to the battlefield, he shook his head. "Nay. They will not return."

Fiadh grew rigid, thinking that at any moment an army would swarm and cut them down. "How can you be sure?"

"There is no one left to kill."

"You survived. Perhaps there are others, and the enemy is waiting for your forces to gather before slaying those who remain."

"There is nobody left, save me."

Fiadh reluctantly craned her neck to look upon the field, flinching as she watched a vulture tear a hunk of flesh from the swollen face of a young soldier. Her stomach convulsed, and she turned away. "Has your memory returned?"

"Aye."

The memories came in waves, bleeding into Gideon's brain in a wash of blades and blood. Remembered screams erupted in his mind, squeals and yelps so awful in their perfect clarity he looked around, frantic, scanning his surroundings. From outside his own tortured thoughts, he heard Fiadh calling to him, but her voice sounded too distant, as though it traveled from across a vale, too far away for him to capture and make sense of. Gideon fell to his knees, hands pressed to his ears, and relived what his mind had kept from him.

Lord Ross Hughes stood in the great hall of Belfirth Castle, his legs braced apart, arms folded, and a scowl stamped upon his bearded face. Brown shoulder-length hair, streaked with grey, capped his massive frame as he towered above the envoy who knelt at his feet. In a voice that thundered through the ample space, he bellowed, "How dare you enter my hall and spew falsehoods!"

The messenger, not much older than a boy, trembled under the glare of this powerful warrior, a man who was known as much for his temper as his prowess in battle. "It is no falsehood, my lord. My master, Lord Crommack, bid me give you this," digging into his tunic, the younger man pulled out a strip of cloth the length of his arm and held it out to Ross, "so that you would know I speak the truth."

Glancing at his sons, Gideon and Doran, he took the material, rubbing his thumb along the complex designs woven into fabric so fine it glided across his skin as though it was little more than air. "Where did your master come by this?" he whispered. His attention fixed on the strange markings which could only have been made by a people long assumed to be dead.

Glancing, then casting his eyes back to the floor, the envoy said, "Lord Crommack took it from the cold, dead hand of his only son."

Ross scrutinized the cloth in his hand, his fingers rubbing it over and over before a noise caught his attention.

Staring through the open doorway into the bailey where his people went about their business, he fixed his sight on a small girl who sat next to a puddle, poking a leaf with the thin tip of a stick as she pushed her makeshift boat across the small span of water. She must be just shy of three years, Ross mused, watching as the child's brother tossed a rock into the puddle, causing mud to splatter on the girl's worn dress. She squealed, flinging her arms up before glaring at her brother, scooping a handful of mud into her fist, and lobbing it at him. Her aim was true, and Ross cracked a smile as he watched the girl's brother mop the muck off his face. His people were the heart of Belfirth, and if war was coming, the kind of war his mind was beginning to evoke, where would they flee? How could he protect them?

"Father?" Gideon asked, his face a mask of worry.

The lord of Belfirth regarded his son, his mouth working for a few moments before clearing it. "They've returned."

"Who?"

"The Aos Sí," he said as Doran and Gideon gasped. "If Lord Crommack is to be taken at his word, and the elves have returned, it can only mean that Rygeil, thought to have been slain in the Great War, has returned."

"Who is this man?" Doran asked.

"Man?" Ross asked, chuckling bitterly, "He is no man. Rygeil was the last of the elven lords. His stronghold, Erabel, lay hidden in the darkest depths of Dorcha Wood, unassailable, and it would remain a stronghold today if our armies hadn't been aided by others who sought to rid this world of that elven filth in the Great Ward." Ross's spiteful laughter interrupted the story as he recalled what his father had told him countless times at his bedside as a boy. "The people of Erabel," he said and spat on the floor, "fought, thinking they could cut through our forces like a scythe. Arrogant to the last," he chuckled. "Beyond the cursed protection of that foul wood, they were no match for our armies, and we cut them down. Every man, woman, and child. All but him. Rygeil. Erabel's lord was not found among the dead, but it was rumored he had been mortally wounded by Lord Darragh's grandfather, Magnar. It appears that was nothing more than speculation."

Quiet shrouded the great hall, broken by the clearing of the envoy's throat. The messenger, who rested his arm upon his upraised knee, looked up at the great lord whose expression had grown stark. "Lord Crommack begs for your aid. He sent a contingent of his soldiers, five hundred strong, into the Felraine Vale after his son, Edan, was found slain with every member of his guard. They haven't returned."

Ross fingered the cloth which still lay across his palm. "And why did Eoghan not join his men?"

A flicker of shame suffused the envoy's face. "He isn't well, my lord."

"I see." Ross looked at his sons, who stood tall and proud at his side. If the elven king had indeed arisen from the dead, then war would surely be upon them all. "How many days since his army was sent?"

"Twelve, my lord."

"Twelve?" He thundered. "It has been twelve days, and I am learning of this threat *now*?" Ross stomped to a large table, kicking a shaggy hound out of his way and grabbing a full pitcher of ale. His throat worked as he downed the liquid, bobbing with every pull until he sucked air and let out a loud belch that echoed in the unnatural quiet. He glared at Lord Crommack's envoy, hands clenching as he eyed the man's neck. "Your master leaves me no choice. None of us are safe if Rygeil has summoned an army to wage war on men. I will amass my soldiers, and we will ride to the Felraine Vale."

"We have no idea of the elves' strength, Father. Perhaps we should look to our borders and not risk sending our full strength marching into the unknown. Let us learn more of Rygeil's numbers while we make safe the keep. If their force is too great, then better to face them from the walls of Belfirth Castle while we wait for the king to raise his armies," Gideon argued.

"And what of Crommack, my sister's husband?" Ross countered. "You would have his people burn while we wring our hands and dally behind our walls? Nay, we must march."

Within a few short hours, Ross's soldiers were ready for battle. Doran and Gideon commanded their own contingents while the core of the army, the Belfirth Guard, would be led by Ross himself. Lord Crommack's envoy rode hard to tell his master of his ally's decision and the need to send reinforcements to assist Belfirth's lord.

Felraine Vale was a land shrouded in superstition. Doran, young at heart for his twenty years and ever the lover of intriguing tales, prodded Gideon as they rode at a sedate pace. "Gwyll tells me that in Felraine lies the place of origin of the Aos Sí, deep magic hidden from the realm of men and from which their people sprung. It is an evil place, he says, thick with fog that can swallow an unwary man in its murkiness until he cannot find his way free of it."

"You shouldn't listen to Gwyll," Gideon admonished, "he wants nothing more than to stoke your fears."

Doran shrugged. "Aye, I know it, but there may be some truth to his tales."

Gideon sighed. "And what truth could there be, brother? Have you seen such things? Have you known of a man to enter that place and never return?"

"Nay, but I have never seen the Southern Sea either, yet I know it exists."

"You cannot think to compare the fanciful tale of a boy who has lived but nineteen years with stalwart men who've traveled beyond our borders and into the greater world. There is much you and I will never see, but yet exists. And then there are the stories spun to frighten children."

"It matters not if children's stories are meant to frighten if at their heart they are true."

"You're hopeless," Gideon chuckled, "….hopeless." Tapping the edge of his boot on his horse's flanks, he urged Aridius onward, leaving his brother with his imaginings behind.

A shrill whistle pierced the air a few leagues before their descent into Felraine Vale. Gideon kicked his steed into a hard canter, weaving through his troops on foot until he caught up to his father. "What is it?"

Ross swept the horizon, squinting in the harsh light. "Our scout has found something. We are awaiting word."

Minutes passed, each seeming interminable. Gideon shifted in his saddle, the soft creak of leather filling the quiet. Doran had joined them and waited by his brother's side. A scout, riding a steed whose coat was white with foam, raced over the hill and toward them, swinging the reins in huge arcs, and slapping them against the poor beast's sides as it spent the last of its energy to reach Ross. Yanking hard on the reins, the horse came to a stop, clots of dirt spraying around its hooves at the sudden halt of its journey.

"My lord," the man panted, "the enemy has amassed just beyond that rise." He pointed to a small cluster of hills that lay just outside of the Felraine Vale. "I didn't truly believe Lord Crommack's man until I saw it with my own eyes. But it is true. The Aos Sí have returned."

Ross's face turned grim. "And their numbers?"

"Some hundreds. I could not get close enough to take a full account, but I would say their army is less than a thousand strong."

A feral smile twitched across Ross' face. "We will obliterate them."

It was decided that Doran and Gideon would split off, each taking their contingent of soldiers around the elven army's location. Ross would lead the Belfirth Guard in a full-frontal attack and shatter the enemy's lines. His sons would sweep in from the flanks and finish them off.

"Shouldn't we wait for Lord Crommack's men?" Gideon asked.

"Nay, we must use the element of surprise and strike now. Our soldiers are better trained than Eoghan's peasants who know no more than how to wave a sword through the air," Ross said snidely. "We will attack and finish this."

Both sons nodded. Gideon slapped Doran on the back. "I'll try to save some elven blood for you to spill, brother."

Doran cocked an eyebrow. "It will be you who will be hunting for something to wet your blade."

Gideon laughed, then urged Aridius into a run, heading

for his men. His father's army began its relentless march, two thousand feet thumping upon the earth in a dull rhythm. Listening to this unmistakable sound of war, blood surged through Gideon's veins, pumping through his muscles, making him feel hot and powerful. Yelling to his legion of a hundred elite soldiers, he broke off from the whole of the army and led them to the west of where the scout had discovered the enemy, where he would flank them.

CHAPTER TWENTY-SEVEN

They emerged from the trees, separating themselves from those woody limbs in a curtain of falling bodies, their coverings having camouflaged them entirely. Springing fleetly to the ground, they rent the air with an eerie battle cry like an animal. The sound grew, doubling and trebling until Gideon covered his ears. As he watched their numbers eclipse those of his men, he realized the scout was wrong. It was an ambush.

"A trap! They're hiding in the trees! Rally to me!" Gideon roared.

Gideon hopped off Aridius, swatting the horse's rump to send him off. He raised his sword, eyes locked on his adversaries, as his men, having been trained under grueling conditions and honed into weapons, formed a tight group.

The Aos Sí came, their footfalls unnaturally muted as they spread out in a deadly fan, arrows whipping through the air in a dizzying blur. Gideon and his men had never seen elves, only heard countless stories of their brutality and cunning. For a few protracted moments, they stood in shock, taking in the forms that came down upon them, so like their own, yet alien with pointed ears and fierce eyes, with foreheads and cheeks painted with complex patterns of green knotwork. Faces of ferocious beauty held no emotion, as their lanky bodies, easily the height of a man, ate up the ground between themselves and Gideon's army. His brain felt frozen in those moments, seeing creatures dressed in cloth that blended with the forest, as though they were part of the trees themselves. They were living nightmares.

An elven arrow whistled past his face and pierced the leather armor of a man at Gideon's side, embedding itself in his flesh with a meaty thud. The soldier crashed to the ground, and all hell broke loose. Metal split the sky and met with blades whose material deflected them with startling ease. Men yelled, grunts of effort filling the spaces between the clang of swords, interspersed by the sickening thunk of more elven arrows finding their mark.

Aos Sí were all around them, and Gideon realized their only hope was to somehow regroup with his father and make a combined stand out in the open field. These woods were the elves' domain. But men, who had spent years in the lists or on the battlefield, panicked, breaking ranks as they tried to flee, only to be picked off.

"Form up!" Gideon shouted. "We must break through their lines! Stick together!"

The staunchest of his men stopped and looked to their leader, their faces wild with fear, and ran to his side. Assembled, they pressed forward as a living mass, shields up, swords swinging.

Gideon shouted, "Hold the line! We must get to my father!"

Aos Sí came at them. Quickly. Ruthlessly. Whooping and shrieking. Screams of pain rapidly filled the air, but those cries were not wholly from hacked limbs and pierced bowels. Fending off the brutal attack of an elven soldier, Gideon glanced to his right and saw Liam, his second in command, writhing on the ground, clutching his arm that bled from a large gash but was whole.

"It burns!" Liam screamed, his body thrashing violently. "Cut it off! Cut it off!" Suddenly he went rigid, back arching grotesquely, before contorting in violent fits. Saliva bubbled out of his mouth as Liam's teeth clenched, jaw locked, eyes bugging, finally going lax after a final spasm.

Gideon's attention snagged on the blade of his enemy, seeing the strange metal gleam with a peculiar light. Swinging viciously, he charged forward, pushing his adversary back while never fully gaining control. He watched the elven blade slice through the air, viewing what could only be interpreted as dark magic imbued within the material itself, reflecting the bloody scene playing out all around him. Soft grunts came from all sides as his men's swords found their mark, but these were few and not fatal. Soon, his soldiers were engulfed.

In a moment of carelessness, Gideon stumbled. His enemy flashed a venomous smile, lunging forward, the blade nicking Gideon's forearm. Slashing in defense, Gideon found his mark, slicing through elven skin and bone. But the moment of triumph was quickly eclipsed by a dagger of pain radiating from his small wound. Staggering backward, Gideon looked at the tiny cut in horror as waves of heat spread. Swinging his arm to his mouth, he wrapped his lips around the wound and sucked, spitting mouthfuls of blood onto the grass. A foul taste filled his tongue, causing him to retch. Around him, he heard the death cries of his men, but they grew faint as the foulness in his mouth leached into his brain, clouding his vision until he fell to the ground in a heap.

Pain lanced through his head as awareness came. He scanned the terrain, only to find himself where he had dropped. The groans of dying men were on all sides as Gideon glanced at the sky. Clouds scuttled by, oblivious to the death beneath them. His head felt heavy, as though his skull were anchored to the ground. Rolling to his side, he looked at the scene. There were bodies everywhere. None of his men was standing. The enemy had moved on, confident in their victory. His heart grew hard as he forced himself to ignore the calls of his dying men. There was naught that he could do to keep them from the Great Mother's embrace.

Clambering to his knees, Gideon looked at the position of the sun, noting little time had passed since he had fallen. Shaking off his abnormal stupor, he staggered to his feet, grabbing his sword to head east to where his father had planned the attack. Pausing mid-stride, he whistled, listening for the sound of Aridius' hooves. A whoosh of relief escaped his chest as the huge warhorse came up the rise, snuffling and nickering at his master's hand.

"Good boy," Gideon rasped, stroking the horse's velvety nose.

It took three attempts to get into the saddle, but eventually, Gideon seated himself, grabbing the reins and kicking

Aridius into a full gallop. Hugging the horse's neck to keep his seat, they raced across the landscape to the sounds of battle.

Cresting a hill, Gideon looked down at his father's army, more than a thousand men strong, being inundated by a raging sea of Aos Sí. His heart fell, there must be two, three thousand at least, and still more were pouring forth from the woods to the north and south. His one aim now was to ride to his kin, raise swords with his brother one last time and die fighting by their father's side. The Lords of Belfirth would make an end worthy of song!

Swinging his reins into Aridius' sides and clenching his lower legs against the horse's middle, he launched into the fray. Everywhere he looked, he saw alien faces twisted with grim purpose and wicked blades cutting through an army who had never known defeat. His father was nowhere to be found, only their family's banner soaked with blood and lying abandoned in the chaos, as elves herded men like sheep into a diminishing circle. Gideon thundered down the rise, lending his voice to the carnage, and screamed for his father.

He found Doran in the distance, still atop his horse, sword striking out with skill Gideon had taught him since they were boys. He wondered for a moment if his brother had also been ambushed, but somehow made it out unscathed to join his father's larger forces. Pride in his sibling filled Gideon, rapidly turning to horror, as a brace of Aos Sí formed a second circle around Doran's men, over-whelming them.

"Doran! Doran, run! Run!" he yelled, willing his voice to carry across the distance. "Doran!" Gideon slogged through the masses. His one aim to reach his brother and die at his side, back to back, swords swinging as they had practiced for hours in the lists. His brother turned then, his eyes finding Gideon for a moment. In that tiny space in time, Gideon saw Doran as a young boy, toddling after him or parrying with his wooden sword, always looking up to his older sibling with hero worship. *Nay… nay not Doran, he must live!* Gideon's mind screamed.

"Doran!" Gideon roared, over and over, kicking Aridius' sides viciously, watching in agony as his brother was swallowed in a mass of bodies.

Gideon leaned into the horse, swinging his sword in a lethal arc as the beast's body slammed into the first challenger. The elf went down in a tumble of graceful limbs before swinging up, bouncing on the balls of his feet and snaking out his arm. All Gideon saw was the glint of sunlight on the strange blade before it slashed in front of Aridius' face. The horse screamed, rearing violently, throwing Gideon off in a tangle of legs where he lay still and stunned before the animal bolted for the hills. Mouth gaping as he struggled to pull breath into his lungs, Gideon listened to the receding drum of his loyal mount's hooves against the earth, quickly becoming too faint above the sounds of men being cut to pieces. A shadow passed over his prone form, blocking the sun as an inhumanly beautiful face, streaked with blood, looked down on him.

Spinning his blade in fanciful swings, the elven soldier gripped the handle and grinned down at Gideon. After letting out a shrill whistle, half a dozen Aos Sí joined him and seized Gideon, hauling him toward a copse of trees. Throwing him to the ground, they stalked toward a solitary elf, greeting their king who stood guarded by two nightmarish beasts. They knelt at his feet, receiving murmured instructions before returning to the battlefield. Gideon watched for a few moments, gaze flicking to the Cù-Sìth who lay next to the elven king, those monsters of legend, that watched him with yellow eyes. Turning away, Gideon shut out the world and wished for nothing more than to join his brother in death.

"This one yet lives, my king," one of the elves said as he toed Gideon's back sometime later.

The Aos Sí king went to Gideon, inspecting him with a critical eye before curling his mouth in a hard smile. He leaned down, wisps of long black hair falling forward to frame pale features with striking green eyes. Caressing Gideon's cheek, then slipping down to cup his chin, he said, "You have the look of a Hughes about you. Are you kin? A son, perhaps?" Gideon tried to pull away, but the elf clenched his hand, forcing him to still. The king closed his eyes and Gideon felt strange and evil tendrils penetrating and probing inside his skull, strolling through his mind, stealing his memories and learning all Gideon ever knew. When the invasion ceased, the elf gave him a cruel smile. "Run along, little lord. Run, run, and find her. She will be drawn to you when you are near. Unable to resist the need to go to you, be with you, follow you," he said, mixing the words with power. "Run, now. Bring her to me."

Muttering a series of incomprehensible words, he pressed a finger to the flesh on Gideon's forehead. Heat bloomed and a blinding flash of light filled Gideon's mind, erupting with such brilliance every thought evaporated, leaving nothing but a vague sense of purpose. The next thing he remembered was being set upon in the meadow outside Dorcha Wood.

"Gideon?" Fiadh asked, her voice evincing the same hushed whispering she used with skittish creatures. Stroking his back in slow circles, she waited for him to come back from wherever he had gone. "Gideon?"

Turning his face to hers, she gasped as she looked into haunted features. "Do you have pain?"

"Nay."

Fiadh caressed his brow, trying to ease the creases that had formed there. "Your memory has returned, has it not?"

"Aye, it has."

"Then you know what happened here?" He nodded. "Who did this?" Fiadh asked in a voice that trembled.

Rigidity seeped into his body like steel as he stood contemplating the ruins of his men. "Elves."

CHAPTER TWENTY-EIGHT

Despite her pleas, Gideon entered the killing grounds and found Doran and the lord of Belfirth. Fiadh watched from a distance as he knelt at their still forms, his chest heaving, though she couldn't hear his sobs, before dragging them from the field and onto an untainted patch of ground. She skirted the battlefield, noticing as she did that the soldiers had been surrounded, their bodies strewn in a circular fashion as though they had been herded and cut down by a force so large in number no army could have stopped it. Hafts of hundreds of elvish arrows pointed to the sky—the only things remaining upright as though those wooden tools of death acted as sentries to the massacre. It made her wonder how Gideon could have escaped. Had he not been with the whole of his army when the fighting began? Was it truly Aos Sí, as Gideon claimed, who had somehow risen from annihilation to wage war against mankind? It was difficult to fathom.

Of the elves, she knew little that could be considered truth, her mother having often changed the subject when it had come about. There were those stories that inevitably made it to her ears, but from those she only gleaned a deep sadness for a people who had been persecuted. To Fiadh, it had always seemed the Aos Sí were collectively hated for no other reason than their difference from humanity. It felt wrong to hate for the sake of hating, and she had never agreed with what she understood were the beliefs of the people of Felmore. She had grown to despise those beliefs, for it was those which had led to the murder of her mother.

In her mind, the Aos Sí had embodied the natural world and a balance within it. From their art to whispers of their magic, they were a mysterious people who had lived in harmony alongside men for generations, until the Great War. How could that be so wrong? How could centuries of peaceful coexistence turn to such blind hatred? Were they truly evil, or was their sordid reputation one of man's making? She shook her head. It was hard to know what to believe, but seeing this massacre, she wondered at the hearts of the Aos Sí.

Breathing through her mouth to keep the stench of decay from enveloping her, Fiadh set aside her questions and knelt at Gideon's side, struggling to look at the mangled forms of his family. Ross's arm had been hacked just below the shoulder, the blade having cut through muscle and bone so that it lay at an unnatural angle upon the ground. His chest had been caved in by some monstrous blow, revealing cavernous wounds which had gone sour over days of exposure and now revealed wriggling masses of worms. Fiadh choked back bile, her body shaking in a battle with her will. Looking upon Doran, her eyes filled with tears. Vultures had gotten to him long before they had found this place, but there was enough of him to recognize. Even through the wide gash that severed his face, she could see a younger Gideon in his features. Fiadh's heart ached as she looked upon these fallen men, the emotions bringing her own loss to the surface in heart-wrenching clarity.

So much death had invaded her peaceful existence since Gideon entered her life. A small but loud part of her wished she had never found him, that she had walked away when Lord Darragh's men attacked him. If she had, perhaps Riona would be living, and she wouldn't be kneeling at this mass grave, looking upon the battered remains of men whose features pulled at her heart because they mirrored one she had grown to care for. Had grown to love. It wasn't fair. If this was what the world outside Dorcha Wood held for those who lived within it, then how could she want to be part of it?

Swallowing her anger and grief, Fiadh touched Gideon's arm, ignoring his flinch at the contact. "I'm so sorry, Gideon."

He nodded. "I have no shovel to bury them. I will not allow the vultures to defile their bodies further."

"We could use rock."

"Aye," he croaked, "though they deserve a lordly funeral. Their bodies resting in the bowels of Belfirth castle with our ancestors, encased in stone until the end of time. Not like this. Not like this."

"Perhaps you can fetch a wagon and men when you reach your land and return for them."

"I don't know if anything will be left of my home," he said desperately.

His words hit her in like a fist. What if the Aos Sí had

left this battlefield and traveled to Belfirth? Fiadh sent up a prayer to Danu, begging for Gideon's people to be safe and unharmed.

"Then they shall have burial mounds until the day you can carry their bodies to your crypt," she said, trying to keep his mind from worry.

Standing, she set off to gather large rocks. Eventually, Gideon joined her efforts, and they spent the time in silence. The only sounds were the gruesome ones of birds feasting on the dead, intermingled with the thump of rocks as they hit the earth. Somewhere, just beyond the morbid scene, Krulan watched and waited.

Gideon's shoulders slumped, his back hunching as though the earth itself was trying to drag him down. Head bowed, he muttered inaudible words, sending them to the forms of his family that now lay under a small cairn of stones. Fiadh stood quietly, giving him privacy as he said his goodbyes, while a dark part of her mind screamed she never had the opportunity with her mother. Seeds of resentment had firmly lodged in her mind, and she was powerless to stop them from gnawing at her. The woods in the west sang to her with each breath of rank air, their music dragging on her mind like an anchor. Krulan called to her, his thoughts a rhythm so like Dorcha Wood, digging into her brain, fertilizing her resentment until it bloomed.

Leave him. Krulan said, his words sinking into her. *He brings nothing but death.*

I care for him. I want to stay by his side, she replied in a mental plea.

Heat crawled up her neck, and she looked at Gideon, catching him staring at her oddly before he turned his head aside. Had she spoken aloud? No. She knew she hadn't, but that look in his eyes felt strange.

Let him find his way alone, Krulan told her. *You must return to Dorcha Wood. It is not safe here. He brings you to your doom.*

I cannot leave, Fiadh said, though within that thought was a deep fear of what she had seen, mingled with a desire to walk away and leave Gideon to his fate. The moment the idea floated across her mind, she felt ashamed and bereft. There stood a man who had just buried his father and brother, whose army had been brutally decimated, and she was thinking of leaving him. What did that say about her character? Fiadh had always felt she was a good person. Now, she had such hate and anger, resentment and grief. It had begun to cloud who she thought she was.

You are my protected, and you must return. His path leads only to blood. Aos Sí blood. Human blood. Your blood.

Fiadh ignored his warnings and brought countless memories of quiet conversations and loving embraces to her mind. She let them sink into her, cleansing her with their purity. *I will stay with him,* she told Krulan.

It was as though Fiadh could feel Krulan's anger, like a bolt of rage aimed at her and Gideon. *You will return.*

Nay, I will not.

There was no response, only a menacing growl that traveled the distance between the two of them and into her body, suffusing it with a warning. As quickly as it came, it was gone. Krulan said nothing more, and it felt as though he had cut himself out of her mind, the absence abrupt. But reaching toward him with her thoughts, she could feel him churning, his emotions tinged with frustration.

I'm sorry, Krulan, she conveyed with her mind. *I cannot go back to that life now. I am bound to him.* Fiadh felt Krulan take in her words, but there was no reply.

Picking up a sharp rock, Gideon drew a series of designs onto the burial mounds, like those of his armor. When he finished, he let his hand linger for a few moments before saying a last farewell. Fiadh straightened as he walked toward her, observing how each step brought a grimace to his face, pain etching lines around his mouth. Glancing at the darkening sky, he said, "We will make camp tonight and set out for Belfirth by morning's light."

They chose a spot far from the bloodied fields, lighting a fire to take away the chill and horrifying images of the day. Spreading out her blanket beside the warmth of the flames, Fiadh lay on her side, eyes half-mast as she watched Gideon poke at the burning wood with a long stick. He had been brooding all evening, withdrawn and refusing to engage in conversation.

Gideon must have felt her stare because he turned to her and asked, "Tell me about the wolf, the one that came to us that day. How is it that it didn't harm you? And the other animals you spoke of, the skunks and the like. You have some affinity with them?"

Surprise filled her face, and for a moment, she didn't know how to reply. "I… I don't know. Animals like me."

He scowled.

She felt flustered and tried to read his face. "I mean," she started, nervously licking her lips, "growing up in the woods, you would have gotten to know all of the wildlife, would you not?"

Gideon made a face and poked at a log. "I haven't seen the like. Until you."

"What are you saying, Gideon?" Fiadh asked, lifting herself up onto her elbow.

Sighing with such weariness, it spilled from his body like a tangible thing, Gideon said, "I don't know. I don't know what I'm saying or thinking anymore. Pay me no mind. Just go to sleep."

Fiadh lowered herself slowly, wondering what he was about, knowing there was more than grief marring his thoughts. The flames licked the wood, the sight of it bringing haunting memories of her mother's body consumed by fire. Tears spilled and soaked into the blanket, but she remained silent, catching the sobs that threatened to erupt. The day's events made her loss feel too raw and unfinished, as though she had been thrust into a nightmare she had no time to process, and it kept pulling at her, heaving her through a forest of misery and death. She wanted it to end. Tomorrow, when they arrived at the border of Gideon's land, she would bid farewell to her past and start anew.

CHAPTER TWENTY-NINE

Gideon nudged her gently, peeling back the edge of her blanket, letting the chill air into her cocoon of warmth. Rolling to the side, Fiadh groaned at the intrusion, but it didn't stop, and, finally, she cracked open her eyes. "Has Father Sun already risen?"

"Aye, and Mother Moon has gone to her rest."

Flopping onto her back, Fiadh squinted at the sky, noting the pastel expanse that held no hint of rain. Her clothes felt damp as she struggled to sit up, weighing her down after collecting moisture throughout the night. Gideon bent low, pain flashing across his face as he gripped his upper thigh muscles and held out his hand. Reaching up, she grasped his fingers and let him pull her upright. She winced, her arms and back sending out flares of pain from her labors the day before. With slow movements, she got to her feet and shuffled to the fire, holding her hands above the dwindling heat from the coals. It was tempting to add more fuel and warm herself, but Fiadh knew Gideon would want to begin the last leg of their journey as soon as they broke their fast.

Gideon held out a handful of dried fruit and nuts. Cupping her hands, she took the offering and ate slowly while her body awakened. "We will come to Belfirth today," he told her.

"How far is it?"

He looked in the direction he had pointed out the day before, a more southerly route from where they camped. "We should arrive by the time the sun is at its highest."

Fiadh looked toward the expanse of land they must cross. The last leg of this journey suddenly felt like it would be the longest stretch. It was frightening, made more so by the massacre they had found the day before. "There is so much violence in your world," she said quietly.

"There is violence in Felmore!" he snapped. "Look at what happened to your mother. Do you think death won't find you if you flee back to your forest?"

She was taken aback by his anger. Gideon looked at her, reason returning as he saw the hurt in her face. He reached for her hand, giving it a small squeeze. She felt his warmth seep into her palm. "I'm sorry. It isn't you I am angry with. The world, our world, is not safe anymore. Somehow, they have survived." He didn't need to say whom he meant. She knew and struggled to come to terms with how she felt about that. "And now," he went on, "the Aos Sí have risen, and all of mankind will be their target. All. And men will fight back, and anything they see which is not..." he paused and looked at her, "... not completely normal, they will attack."

"Perhaps we would be safer in Dorcha Wood," she offered. "I was safe there, protected."

"By whom? Your creatures? The squirrels? Your wolf?"

Her eyes sparked. "If not for those *creatures*, you wouldn't be alive today."

Gideon scoffed, the sound ugly and discordant in that still surrounding. "I doubt that."

"Who do you think carried your body to my home? Me? I couldn't manage such a feat on my own."

Waving his hand at Fiadh, he said, "It matters not. Elves are at war with men. Do you know what happens to the weak who find themselves at the mercy of the strong?"

"Don't try to frighten me, Gideon. I am not so weak as you think," she scolded, anger infused in every syllable.

"Aye, mayhap you are not," he said, holding her gaze in a way, that for the first time, did not feel wholly pleasant.

"Gideon, we are from different worlds, different lives, truly, I… I do not know what I am, but the one thing that I do know is, whatever I am… I am yours."

Gideon looked at her, his face crumpling. "And I am yours." Wrapping her in his arms, she felt him breathe in her scent as he pressed his nose to her hair. "I'm sorry, Fiadh, forgive… forgive me."

"I do."

Grasping her shoulders in strong but gentle hands, he pleaded, "If aught happened to you…" he took a deep breath, "I couldn't live with myself. I've lost everyone… everyone… but I found *you.*"

Within that declaration, she saw he had fallen in love with her and, until that moment, she hadn't known what it would look like. Fiadh's heart stirred, pulled by the weight of his words, knowing there was so much of her he didn't understand, and feeling the desire to let it go. Before her was a man who had reshaped her life, in ways which left her aching and alone, but also touched in new and strange ways. Could she ever go back to how it had been before he had come crashing into it? Logic told her no. She leaned her head into his chest, feeling his arms wrap around her. It felt good.

"We could have a future together," he whispered.

"Aye." And for a few moments, she could picture it, sitting next to him in a great hall while the faces of his people drifted past with joy at the sight of their union. But then the image blurred, the walls of that large expanse closing in on her, keeping her within their immovable embrace. "I will miss the freedom of my youth," she said softly.

"Do you think I would keep you, prisoner, in my castle? Cast you into the dungeons?" he asked, chagrinned. "You would be free to roam, as you have always done."

"Would I?"

He nodded. "In time, aye, but not when there is a threat as there is now."

Her face clouded over. "I..." she began, pausing as she collected herself. "I have many fears for the future and longings for what I lost." He opened his mouth, but she touched his lips, pressing lightly. "I cannot know if I will fit into your life and with your people. But...I am willing to try. I've... I've grown very fond of you, and I think Mother would have wanted me to make this choice. I think she would approve."

Joy, tinged with a weight of sorrow for the lives he had

lost, flooded his features. "You have given me a great gift, Fiadh. Let us finish this journey and go home."

Within the recesses of a copse of trees just beyond their site, she heard the low rumble of Krulan's growl. Gideon glanced in that direction, making her heart skitter, then packed up their belongings and handed Fiadh her burden. She slung it over her shoulders, casting glances into the trees, searching for Krulan, her eyes darting from dark space to dark space. Would Krulan let her stay with Gideon? The answer, it seemed, resonated in a soft snarl that drifted through the branches and into her heart.

CHAPTER THIRTY

Cresting the rise at the border of Gideon's land, Fiadh sucked in a breath. It was a beautiful stronghold, set beneath the breast of a craggy mountain. Spanning the whole of the land were rolling fields dotted with sheep, though no shepherds tended them from her vantage point, and interspersed were thatched cottages with well-traveled dirt roads leading to the demesne itself and numerous outbuildings. No smoke poured from the roof of the castle or peasant's huts to mar the sky and taint the air. In fact, the villagers were wholly absent from the idyllic scene. All tucked away in their homes, no doubt, she mused, passing the noon hour with a hearty meal. It was utterly tranquil, this small world of humanity, set within the shadow of Viliock Mountain. The sight of it caused a slight pang in her chest. She could well imagine walking among the huts, sharing her knowledge of herbs and animal ways with the locals. In the back of her mind, she couldn't help wondering if that was a fantasy, quickly dispelled by a cruel word or vicious rumor.

Turning her head, Fiadh watched as Gideon fell to his knees, leaning forward to press his forehead to the ground in supplication. "Blessings on you, Great Mother, for protecting my people," he whispered.

Rising, Gideon clasped Fiadh's hand, tugging her as he descended the hill. With a careless step, her foot snagged on a root, and she tripped, landing hard on her knees with a yelp.

"Are you al—"

Fiadh looked at Gideon, his mouth frozen mid-word. Turning to see what he was gaping at, she watched in horror as Krulan separated himself from the darkness of over-hanging branches.

"Run!" Gideon roared, grabbing her arm so forcefully she toppled backward, rolling down the hill a few paces before hitting the point of a rock jutting from the ground. She cried out, cupping her side where a bruise was sure to form. As the sound of her cry still hung in the air, a vicious snarl tore through the hills.

"Run, Fiadh!" Gideon screamed, pulling his sword from its sheath and stepping between her and the beast.

Krulan launched himself at Gideon, the animal's powerful limbs tearing huge clods of dirt from the earth and throwing them into the air in showers of rock and soil.

Fiadh screamed, her mind pleading with Krulan to stop, but he came at Gideon, a relentless force of muscle and teeth. Fiadh watched, horrified, as the man she had grown to love raised his sword, spreading his legs in the stance of a warrior. He showed no fear, years of training having severed thoughts of fleeing when faced with a mortal enemy. Time slowed, each of Krulan's enormous strides stretching out as he ate up the distance, so she could see his sharp nails dig ruts in the ground and watch as flecks of bloodthirsty drool sprayed out behind him. Peeling back the lips of his muzzle, Krulan growled, his serrated teeth winking in the dark mass of his fur. Yellow eyes fixed on Gideon's throat as he leaped, his body launching itself with impossible speed.

Gideon's sword flew, spinning in the air before landing with a thunk. He was thrown back, his body striking the ground so forcefully his head bounced off the earth. Fiadh screamed, scrambling to her knees and crawling toward Gideon's side. She could see his mouth gaping open for a moment, as though the fall had knocked the breath from his lungs, before Krulan spread his jaw, spittle flying in foamy clots. Fiadh found her feet then, leaping toward Krulan as his mouth clamped onto Gideon's throat.

"No! No!" she screamed, tugging at his neck to pull him away. She could smell that sweet, rancid scent of his breath, feel the strange coarse fur. Growls erupted from Krulan's chest, followed by a jab into her mind.

He dies!

"No!" she begged, her arms shaking as she tugged at his massive form. "Krulan, please!" Sobs wracked her body. "Please don't kill him. Please," she begged in a voice gone hoarse. "Krulan, don't do this."

Fiadh felt the moment he opened his jaw. *For you, he is spared.*

Thank you, she said, pushing at his body as though she had the strength to move it. Krulan stood rooted for a moment, his massive paws pinning Gideon to the ground. *I must see to him,* she pleaded, shoving. *Please.*

With a low growl, Krulan stepped aside, moving a few

paces away but not leaving. Fiadh glanced at him before turning all her attention to the man who lay choking on the grass. His body turned on its side as spasms of coughing rattled his form. She pushed his hair and tunic aside, inspecting his neck. Tiny pools of blood welled at irregular points, though none were deep enough to do any lasting harm. Relief filled her, and she reached down, helping Gideon sit up.

He looked at her, eyes wild, heart racing before his gaze fell on Krulan. Betrayal suffused his features, washing away the physical pain and fear, leaving behind an expression she had never seen before that moment. Gideon pulled his attention away from Krulan and glared at her. What she saw made her heart twist. "Gideon, I can explain."

Looking from one to the other, darkness fell across his face. "Can you? Do you know what that is?" he snarled, thrusting his finger toward Krulan. Sitting straighter, he laughed, the sound jarring and cruel. "Of course, you know what he is. Like mother, like daughter, eh?"

"That's not fair," she pleaded, "you don't understand."

"Don't I?" Rising slowly, his body unfurled before her, becoming something hard and commanding. Cold. "I think I do understand. I think I finally understand. You are one of them!"

"One of what?" she begged but already knew the answer. She just had to hear him say it.

"An Aos Sí witch," he sneered, a glob of spit hitting her in the face following his damning pronouncement.

Fiadh flinched, her heart shriveling in her chest. Krulan, having felt her turmoil, growled and stalked forward, head lowered, fur bristling. "Don't," she sobbed, though it wasn't clear whom she meant. Forcing herself to stare Gideon in the face, she begged, "Please, Gideon."

"Have you any idea what that monster is?" She nodded, but he continued. "The Cù-Sìth are Aos Sí hounds, guardians of their kingdoms and murderous beasts!" he screamed at her, making a sign to ward off the evil he saw standing before him. "The Aos Sí are evil, spawned by dark magic and grown into twisted creatures who want nothing more than to see mankind obliterated. And you're one of them!" he roared, grabbing his fallen sword and pointing it at Fiadh's heart. "I should kill you where you stand before you bring more ruin on my people, you *witch*!" His face twisted in an ugly sneer. "I see it now, the elf king's plan, he would have you sneak inside the walls of Belfith Castle, poison our wells, destroy us from within. What need for him to spend his soldiers' lives storming our walls when you will do all for him?"

Anguish tore from her throat, spilling out of her mouth in a flood of denial, as Krulan's shadow fell over her. She felt the heat of his body, heard the low rumble of fury trembling through his chest. His rage battered her, the taste of blood, a tang in her mouth, as she shared his savagery through their mingling thoughts. "I am not evil, Gideon," Fiadh wept, "I am not an elven witch."

"Lies!" he bellowed, his voice echoing off the hills. "Leave before I kill you both."

Shock and heart-wrenching betrayal suffused her mind. "Gideon."

He raised his sword. Krulan let out a nasty snarl, wickedly long teeth gleaming through his dark muzzle, as he pushed Fiadh aside. She grabbed the scruff of his neck to hold him back, though she was no match for his strength if he chose to lunge. Grief-stricken, Fiadh stared at Gideon, drinking him in, accepting what she saw before her. The man she had fallen in love with was gone, vanished the moment Krulan stepped from the shadows. The moment when who she really was, came into the light. Who stood before her now was a stranger. Angry and embittered. Vengeful and twisted. Her heart gave a violent galumph, wrenching itself into two jagged pieces, severing the part of her which had reached for this man and the future he held. Cleaved, that small piece shriveled, hastened by the hatred filling his features as Gideon glowered at her.

Krulan knelt down next to Fiadh, coaxing her to climb upon his back. With shaking hands, she reached for him, never taking her eyes off Gideon, hoping to see some crack in his resolve, some of the warmth they had shared over the last span of days. Krulan rose, a baleful stare boring into Gideon with a warning. Fiadh clutched fistfuls of his pelt, feeling the coarser hairs poking into her palms.

Her heart sank as she watched Gideon strengthen his resolve. "Leave and never return. If I see you again… I'll kill you."

Fiadh wept and turned away from his hatred. Krulan uttered a scathing rebuke, though Gideon would hear only the sound of a mindless beast. Leaning forward, she buried her face in Krulan's fur, feeling his body coil and spring, taking huge strides which ate up the land until Gideon was but a memory, standing on that bluff, alone.

The ground they had traveled for days became a blur as Krulan raced across the hills, ignoring the trees which had kept him hidden on their journey to Belfirth. His gait never slowed, his breathing never labored, and despite her added weight, his strength seemed boundless. The tears, which had run so freely, had stopped, leaving an aching hole in her chest. Fiadh clutched her woolen dress, bunching the fabric in her fist as she held onto Krulan's thick pelt. Her knuckles beat against her heart in time with his giant strides, a reminder she still lived despite the pain.

On the horizon, a lone figure watched their progress. He sat upon a creature lost to mankind, a beast that had passed from legend and into that forgotten realm. Long, starkly pale hair, braided for war, framed a face of alabaster skin. Violet eyes homed in on the figures racing across the landscape, fixating on the form gripping the back of the Cù-Sìth. Murmuring in a language not heard for generations of men, he spoke to the beast on whose back he perched, urging the animal to follow. The creature swung its head, a thick horn protruding from between its ears, dark at the base, gradually becoming white as the blackness bled out, leaving the deadly tip nearly translucent atop its equine face. Heeding its rider, the unicorn bobbed his head, striking a broad shaggy hoof on the ground before lunging forward in an enormous bound.

Krulan, sensing the rider bearing down on them, picked up his grueling pace. He ran. Back to Dorcha Wood. Into its heart. To Erabel.

Fiadh's story will continue in book two of the Daughter of Erabel series:

≈

Blood of the Lost Kingdom

My Irish blood sings to me as I write, and I love infusing my books with lore from this fascinating culture. The *Daughter of Erabel* series is ripe with references to creatures from Irish mythology. The Cù-Sìth, also known as Cú Sídhe, are prominent in Scottish and Irish folklore. They are said to be faery hounds, guardians of faery kingdoms and bringers of death. They are often described as the size of small horses with green and black fur. Some legends say that if you hear the howl of one of these hounds, death is coming.

For this series, I wanted to take the foundational ideas of the Cù-Sìth and bring them to life in a way that gives these creatures depth. Krulan and his pack represent a complex society. They are thoughtful and highly intelligent, not the beasts of nightmares from many Irish legends. In addition to the Cù-Sìth, other creatures, like the gruagach (often referred to as brownies) and slaugh, are mentioned, though it is in *Blood of the Lost Kingdom* that you will be formally introduced to these creatures.

Each book in the *Daughter of Erabel* series features unique

Celtic knotwork. In *The Girl of Dorcha Wood*, you see the Tree of Life. This is one of the most common knots seen in Celtic jewelry and artwork and harkens back to the ancient Celts (Druids) who had a great affinity for trees, especially oak. The Tree of Life knot has many meanings, but at its heart is the belief that trees represent forces that take care of life on earth. In the knotwork itself, you will see the traditional continuous knots prevalent in Celtic art. This reflects the never-ending cycle of life. In the Tree of Life knot, the roots reach into the ground, representing the lower world, and the branches reach into the air, representing the upper world. The trunk is the realm of earth. These worlds are joined in an eternal loop.

As you progress through the series, you will be introduced to reinvented creatures from Irish legend and Celtic knots that reflect core themes in each book. I hope you enjoy delving into a unique world of Irish mythology.

ACKNOWLEDGMENTS

As with many of my books, it all begins with an opening scene and, from those initial words, a story is born. *The Girl of Dorcha Wood* is my first foray into historical fantasy, and without the love and support of family and friends, it may have gathered proverbial dust on my laptop.

First and foremost, I thank my family for standing by me, or leaving me in my writing chair for hours, as I took an idea and turned it into what will become a four-book series. My husband sat through hours of babbling about characters and storylines and still managed to smile and bring me a glass of wine or a plate of snacks. He was my cheerleader throughout, and I love him for his unconditional support as I went through the ups and downs of the writing process. The fact that he didn't wish for a mute button as I rambled about writing is a testament to his character!

Throughout the process, my sons gave me time and quiet to camp in the living room, tapping away on the keys, and never begrudged me the hours I needed. I enjoyed making them snicker as I whined about deadlines, groaned about writing a blurb, or listened to pronunciations of Irish words over and over. Their hugs got me through the rough patches, and their belief in me gave me wings.

David, my editor, knows me so well! He always takes what I give him and helps me thread it together with depth and strength. I loved his Conan recommendations for fight scenes and did a happy dance as he suggested I read Pillars of the Earth - little did he know at the time that I read it every couple of years!

JD, my cover designer extraordinaire, leaves me in awe as he takes my ideas, breathing life into them until they are positively stunning. I am so thankful I found him and have been privileged to work with JD on each of my books!

Vanessa and Christina, you are the founders and CEOs of my fan club! How many times have I blathered on about the book? Or shown you versions of the cover? Or sent you manuscripts? I don't even know. Counting those instances would be mathematical, and I'm not math-ing right now! What I do know is that you always humored me and gave me the nudge I needed to keep moving along and chasing that dream.

ABOUT THE AUTHOR

Kristin Ward is an award-winning author from Connecticut. She embraces her inner nerd regularly, geeking out with SciFi flicks or quoting 80s movies while expecting those around her to chime in with appropriate rejoinders. As a nature freak, she can be found wandering the woods - she may be lost, so please stop and ask if you see her - or chilling in her yard with all manner of furry and feathered friends. Often referred to as a unicorn by colleagues, in reality, the horn was removed years ago, leaving only a mild imprint that can be seen if she tilts her head just right. A lifelong lover of books and writing, she dreamed of becoming an author for thirty years but lazed about and didn't publish anything until 2018. Her debut novel, **After the Green Withered**, is the first of other stuff you should probably read.

To learn more, visit kristinwardauthor.com!

BLOOD OF THE LOST KINGDOM

BOOK TWO OF THE DAUGHTER OF ERABEL

The candle guttered, its flame flickering atop the waxen heart—a sickly yellow mass made from the fat of a newborn. Crackles and pops erupted in the darkness, in time with the echo of that squalling innocent. The ghostly wails, so like the cries of Haegna as she pleaded from beyond the dank cell, begging for a word, a taste.

The mage rocked, muttering in cadences strange and sinister, his body swaying with words of power. His pale face lay shrouded in a cloak so black it melted into the darkness, concealing all but the skeletal hands that sifted through runes strewn about the single table of the dank cell. A lone figure sat upon a plush chair brought into that foul space, tucked into the damp corner of slick rock and rusted iron— far enough away from the acrid stench of the mage whose captivity did not allow for bathing. Eyes bore into the rocking form as though the observer could learn the secrets of that dark magic simply by watching as they were spun from nothing.

Slamming his hands upon the rough wood, Xander

lunged backward, the tendons in his neck bursting in stark relief as wide eyes stared into the nothingness above him. His voice rose, seeming to double and treble, growing louder, the din forcing the man who sat but a short distance away to cover his ears. Words spat from a mouth of rotted teeth, vile and vicious, curling in the air, thick with meaning and malice.

The noises reached an impossible crescendo as the watcher pressed his fists against his skull to escape them.

And then, abruptly, it stopped.

Silence smothered every sound, even the rapid breathing of the figure whose aching fists fell to his lap. Slumping upon on his worn stool, Xander dropped his head, the hood of his cloak wrapped itself around his face, embracing its master like a thing half alive. The watcher flexed fingers that had grown rigid under the onslaught of what had transpired only moments before.

In an otherworldly voice, the mage hissed, "The Aos Sí have risen. Look to Dorcha Wood. The daughter of Erabel has come. But do not fool thyself into thinking she is easy prey. The Cù-Sìth protect her, and her lost kin are assembling. They are of one mind. One purpose."

"Tell me," snarled Lord Darragh.

"Vengeance."